# TALES FROM
# Storyland

*Illustrated by*
Jeremy Bays, Natalie Bould, Lynn Breeze, Anna Cattermole,
Maureen Galvani, Mary Hall, Virginia Margerison, Paula Martyr, Julia Oliver,
Martin Orme, Sara Silcock, Gillian Toft, Charlie Anne Turner, Kerry Vaughan,
Jenny Williams, Kirsty Wilson

*Designed by* Louise Millar

First published in 1998 by
PARRAGON
13 Whiteladies Road
Clifton
Bristol BS8 1PB

Copyright © 1998 Parragon

Created and produced for Parragon by
Linda Watters Book Packaging
8 Trent Close
Shenley
Herts WD7 9HX

ISBN 0-75252-839-4

Printed in Italy

# TALES FROM
# Storyland

*Written by*
Derek Hall, Alison Morris and Louisa Somerville

PARRAGON

# Contents

# Mr Mole Gets Lost

Mr Mole poked his little black nose out from the top of one of his mole hills and gave a great big sniff of the air. Then he sniffed again. And then a third time just to make sure. "Oh dear," he thought, "it smells like it's going to rain."

Mr Mole didn't like the rain one bit. Every time he got caught in the rain his plush little velvet fur coat got all wet and drippy, and he left muddy footprints all over his underground burrow. But worse still, the rain got in through the holes in his mole hills and then everything got all soggy and took days to dry out.

Well, the skies got darker and darker, and very soon little spots of rain began to fall. Then the spots became bigger. And then bigger still. Before long, all you could see before your eyes were big, straight rods of rain bouncing off the leaves on the trees, pounding the ground and turning everything muddy and wet.

Mr Mole had never seen rain like it. He sat in his burrow in the middle of the meadow wishing it would stop. But it just kept raining and raining. Soon the rain started entering his burrow. First it went drip, drip, drip through the holes in his mole hills, and then it became a little river of water in the bottom of his burrow. Then the little river became a bigger, faster-flowing river and suddenly Mr Mole was being washed along by it. Through the tunnels of his burrow he went, this way and then that, as the water gushed and poured through his underground home.

The next thing he knew he was being washed out of his burrow completely as the rain water carried him off down the meadow. Down he went, not knowing which way up he was or where he was going. Now he was being washed through the woods at the bottom of the meadow, but still the water carried him on, bouncing and turning him until he was dizzy and gasping for breath.

Suddenly, he came to a halt. The rain water gurgled and trickled around him and then flowed onwards, as he found himself stuck firmly in the branches of a bush. "Oh dear," Mr Mole said as he got himself free. "Goodness me, where can I be?" he thought. Mr Mole looked around him, but being a very short-sighted mole – as most moles are – he couldn't make out any of the places that were familiar to him. Worse still, he couldn't smell any smells that were familiar to him. He was completely lost, far from home, and had no idea how to get back again. Now, to make things worse, it was starting to get dark.

"Woo-oo-oo-oo-oo!" said a voice suddenly. Mr Mole nearly jumped out of his moleskin with fright. "I wouldn't stay here if I were you," said the voice again. Mr Mole looked up and found himself face to face with an enormous owl. "Don't you know it's not safe in the woods at night?" asked the owl. "There are snakes and foxes and weasels and all sorts of nasty creatures that you really wouldn't like to meet."

"Oh dear!" was all Mr Mole could think of saying. He told the owl of his terrible watery journey and how he was lost and didn't know how to get back home again.

"You need to talk to Polly Pigeon," said the owl. "She is a homing pigeon and she lives near your meadow. She can show you the way home. But we'll have to find her first. Stay close to me, mind, and look out for those snakes, foxes and weasels I told you about."

Mr Mole didn't need telling twice. He stayed so close to the kindly owl that every time the owl stopped or turned round to talk to Mr Mole, Mr Mole bumped right into him!

Through the dark, dangerous woods they went. Every now and again, there would be an unfriendly noise, such as a deep growl or a hiss, coming from the dense, tangled trees, but Mr Mole didn't want to think about that too much, so he just made sure that he never lost sight of the owl.

Finally, just when Mr Mole thought that he couldn't go a step further, they came to a halt by an old elm tree.

"Hallo-oooo," called the owl.

They were in luck. Polly Pigeon was waking up, and they found her just in time for she was about to continue her journey home.

"Please," said Mr Mole, "I'm afraid I'm terribly lost and don't know how to get back to my meadow. Will you take me there?"

"Of course I will," said Polly Pigeon. "We'd better let you rest here a while first, though. But we must go before it gets light."

So Mr Mole was soon trudging wearily back to his meadow, following as closely behind Polly Pigeon as he was able. Just as the first rays of sun lit the morning sky, Mr Mole smelled a very familiar smell. It was his meadow! He was almost home!

Soon, he was back in his own burrow. It was so wet and muddy, however, that the first thing he did was build some new tunnels higher up the meadow so that the rain wouldn't wash down into them so easily. Then he settled down to eat one of his supplies of worms, and fell into a deep, well-earned slumber.

# Granny Casts a Spell

Susie was very fond of her Granny. Each day, when Susie got home from school, Granny was always there sitting by the fire knitting. Granny knitted so fast that sometimes it seemed as though the knitting needles sparked in the firelight.

"Do you know," Granny would say, "that I'm really a witch?" Susie always laughed when Granny said that because she didn't look at all like a witch. She had a smiling face and kind eyes and she never wore black. Not ever. When Granny wasn't looking, Susie would take a peek inside her wardrobe just in case she might find a broomstick or a witch's hat. But she never found so much as a book of spells.

"I don't believe you're a witch," said Susie.

"I am," replied Granny, "and I'll cast a spell one day. You'll know when that day comes, for my needles will start to knit by themselves." After that, Susie kept a careful watch over Granny's needles, but they always lay quite still in the basket of knitting.

One day, Susie was playing in her garden when she heard the sound of weeping. The sound seemed to be coming from under the old tree in the corner. She walked towards the tree and as she did so the crying noise got louder, but she could not see anyone there. Then she looked down at her feet and there – sitting on a mossy stone – was a tiny little man. He was neatly dressed in a yellow velvet waistcoat and knickerbockers. On his feet were beautiful, shiny, buckled shoes, and a three-cornered hat with a wren's feather in it trembled on his shaking head. When the little man saw Susie, he stopped crying and started to dab his eyes with a fine lace handkerchief.

"Whatever can the matter be?" asked Susie, crouching down.

"Oh dear, oh dear!" sobbed the little man, "I am the fairy princess's tailor and she has asked me to make her a lovely gown to wear to the May Ball tonight, but a wicked elf has played a

13

trick on me and turned all my fine gossamer fabric into bats' wings. Now I shall never be able to make the princess's gown and she will be very angry with me." He started to cry again.

"Don't cry!" said Susie. "I'm sure I can help. My Granny's got a sewing basket full of odds and ends. I'll see if she's got anything nice for a party dress. I'm sure she won't mind sparing some – after all, you won't need much," she said. At that, the little man looked a bit more cheerful.

"Wait here," said Susie, "while I run indoors and see." She ran up the garden path and in through the back door.

"Granny, Granny!" she called. She ran into the sitting room expecting to find Granny knitting by the fire. But Granny had her eyes closed and she was whispering to herself. On her lap was her knitting – and the needles were moving all by themselves, so that the yarn danced up and down on the old lady's knees.

For a moment, Susie was too astounded to move. Then she thought, "I hope Granny's not casting a bad spell. I'd better make sure the little tailor is alright."

She ran back down the garden path and there under the tree sat the tailor, surrounded by a great pile of gorgeous gossamer, shining in the sunlight.

"I've never seen such fine material – ever!" he exclaimed. "But where did it come from? I just closed my eyes to dab them with my hanky and when I opened them again – there it was!"

"I don't know," said Susie, "but I think my Granny might have had something to do with it."

"Well, I'd never be able to thank her enough," said the tailor. "For now I shall be able to make the finest gown in the whole of fairyland. The princess will dance the night away in the prettiest dress there ever was." He paused and then went on, "I'm also indebted to you, for it was you who helped me in the first place. I would like it very much if you came to the May Ball, too."

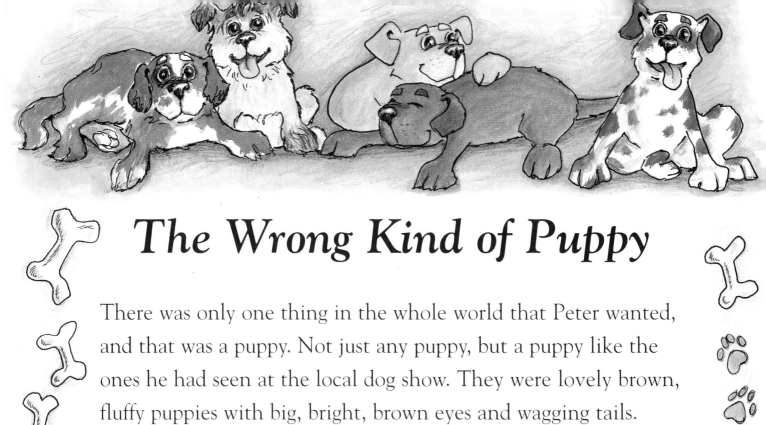

# The Wrong Kind of Puppy

There was only one thing in the whole world that Peter wanted, and that was a puppy. Not just any puppy, but a puppy like the ones he had seen at the local dog show. They were lovely brown, fluffy puppies with big, bright, brown eyes and wagging tails. Peter had spent all day at the show stroking the puppies, and they had spent all their time on their back legs wanting to be stroked even more!

Best of all, Peter's parents had promised him a puppy of his very own for his birthday. He could hardly wait. "Please can we get one like those lovely brown ones we saw at the dog show?" he pleaded.

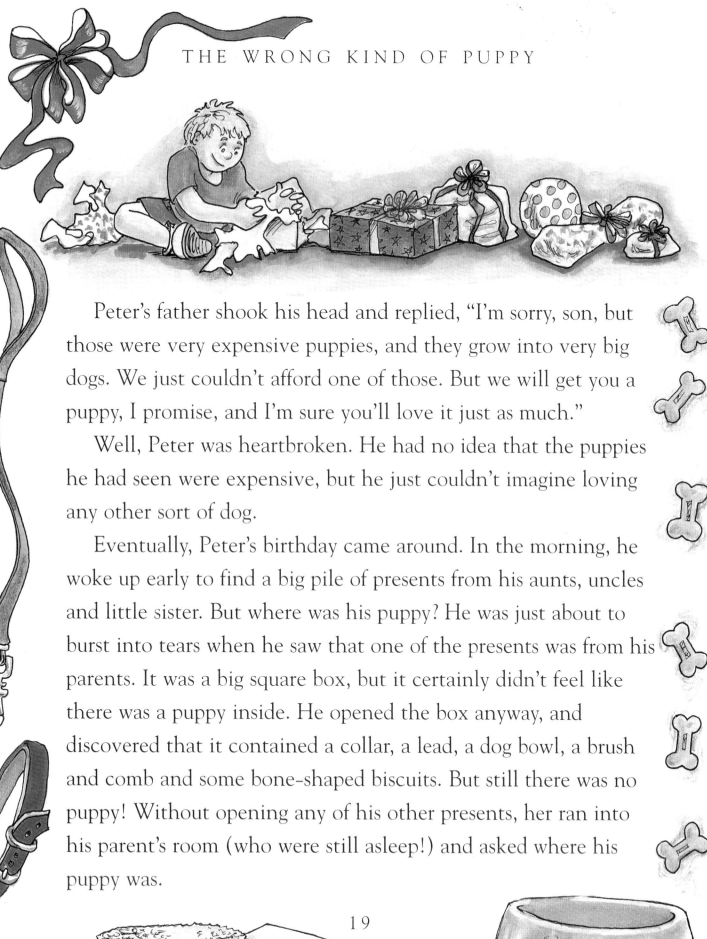

Peter's father shook his head and replied, "I'm sorry, son, but those were very expensive puppies, and they grow into very big dogs. We just couldn't afford one of those. But we will get you a puppy, I promise, and I'm sure you'll love it just as much."

Well, Peter was heartbroken. He had no idea that the puppies he had seen were expensive, but he just couldn't imagine loving any other sort of dog.

Eventually, Peter's birthday came around. In the morning, he woke up early to find a big pile of presents from his aunts, uncles and little sister. But where was his puppy? He was just about to burst into tears when he saw that one of the presents was from his parents. It was a big square box, but it certainly didn't feel like there was a puppy inside. He opened the box anyway, and discovered that it contained a collar, a lead, a dog bowl, a brush and comb and some bone-shaped biscuits. But still there was no puppy! Without opening any of his other presents, her ran into his parent's room (who were still asleep!) and asked where his puppy was.

19

"We have to go and collect it today," said his mother. "We've chosen you a lovely little puppy from the dogs' home that desperately needed a new family to look after it. We can go and get it as soon as we've had breakfast."

Peter was much too excited to eat any breakfast, of course, and spent the next half hour saying, "Can we go yet?" Eventually everyone was ready, and they all climbed into the car for the journey to the dogs' home. Peter sat in the back clutching the lead and hoping it wouldn't be too long before there was a puppy attached to the other end of it!

Soon they reached the dogs' home, and one of the kennel maids took them to where Peter's puppy was being kept. But when Peter first set eyes on the puppy, his heart sank. This wasn't anything like the sort of puppy he had wanted. Instead of being brown and fluffy and bouncy, this puppy was tiny and scraggy and timid. When it saw Peter and his family approach, it gave a little wag of its tail but then just stood in its cage whimpering.

Now Peter had been taught by his parents that you must never be ungrateful for presents, even if they aren't exactly what you wanted. So although he was very disappointed, he reached out and stroked the puppy. The little scruffy puppy timidly approached Peter, licked his hand, and then ran off into the corner of the cage.

"He'll soon get used to you," said the kennel maid brightly. "Come on, Rags, time to go to your new home." And with that, she lifted the little puppy up and placed him in Peter's arms.

All the way home, the little puppy sat quietly in Peter's arms, occasionally trembling. Now and again he looked up at Peter with his big, soft eyes.

When they got Rags home, he was so frightened that he ran and hid under the curtains. Peter wondered how he was going to be able to play with such a timid friend.

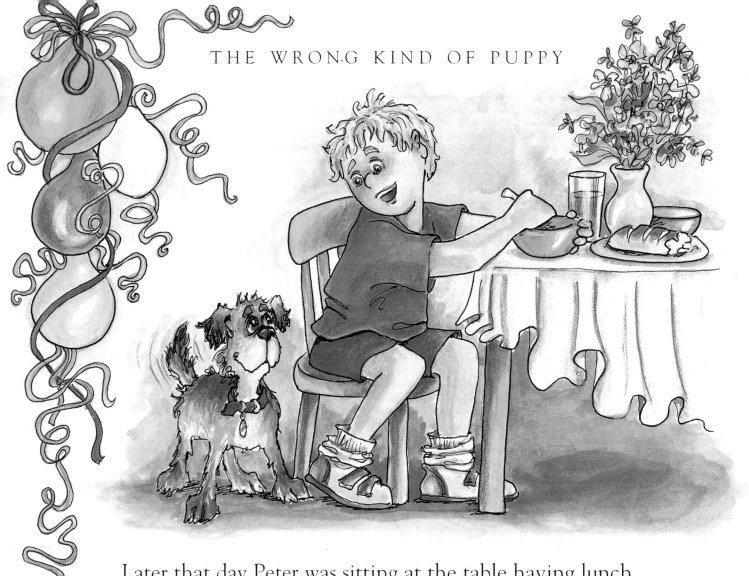

Later that day Peter was sitting at the table having lunch when he felt something cold and wet against his leg; it was Rags's nose. He peered down to see Rags looking up at him, his tail wagging backwards and forwards. "He's looking a bit happier now," said Peter's father. "It will only be a matter of time before he feels really at home here."

The next morning, Peter hurried downstairs as soon as he awoke to say good morning to Rags – because the truth was, although Rags wasn't quite like the puppy he had expected, he was really getting very fond of him.

Rags jumped out of his basket when he saw Peter, his tail wagging furiously. "He's quite a waggy dog after all," thought Peter. Then Rags picked up his ball and began to play with it. Every time Peter tried to take it, Rags scurried off with a wag of his tail, looking round to make sure that Peter was chasing him. He seemed to like playing after all!

As the days went by, Rags seemed to grow more and more playful. He would jump up and greet his family with a big lick and a wagging tail, he always wanted to go for walks and to play, and he was very quick to learn tricks.

Peter just couldn't believe how much Rags had changed from the timid little creature in the dogs' home to the happy, playful puppy he was now – all thanks to a little love and care.

But the most curious thing of all was the puppy's appearance. He had now grown a beautiful, fluffy coat and, if Peter wasn't very much mistaken, it was quite brown, too. And it matched the colour of his big, brown eyes.

# The Invisible Imp

One day, Sarah Jones was pegging out her washing. It was a lovely day and she was looking forward to visiting her friend Rose. "I'll just get this washing on the line while the sun's shining," she said to herself, "and then I'll be on my way."

After a while, she stopped and looked down into the basket. "That's very peculiar!" she thought. "I know I've already pegged out that green shirt and there it is back in the basket." She carried on pegging out the clothes. Now she shook her head in disbelief. For although she had been working away for quite a while, the basket of washing was still full and there was almost nothing on the line! She began to get quite cross, for she was going to be late getting to Rose's house.

Try as she might, she just could not get that washing pegged. In the end, she had to leave the basket of wet washing and run to Rose's house.

"I'm so sorry I'm late, Rose," she gasped, all out of breath from running. Sarah told Rose all about what had happened.

"Well," said Rose, "that's a strange coincidence. I was baking some cakes for us to have for tea. Every time I put them in the oven and turned away, they were out of the oven and on the table again! In the end I had to stand guard over them – which reminds me, they were just beginning to cook nicely when you knocked on the door."

The two women went into Rose's kitchen and there were the cakes, sitting on the table again, half-cooked. "Now they're ruined!" cried Rose. "Whatever shall we do?"

At that moment, there was a noise in the street. Rose and Sarah looked out of the window to see Elmer, the postman, surrounded by a crowd of people all shouting and waving envelopes in the air. The two women ran out into the street. "What's going on?" they cried.

"Elmer's given us all the wrong post," said Rose's neighbour, Dora. "He's normally so reliable, but this morning he seems to have gone completely crazy. Now we've got to sort out all the mail for him."

"I don't know what's happened," wailed Elmer in anguish. "I'm sure I posted all the letters through the right doors."

"Well," said Sarah, "Rose and I have also found strange things happening to us this morning." She told the crowd their stories. Everyone forgave Elmer when they realised it wasn't his fault, but they were still truly mystified as to what – or who – could have caused all these problems.

But that wasn't the end of it. Oh no, indeed! The butcher's wife served her family mutton stew, but when she lifted the lid the family heard a bleating sound and a little lamb leaped out of the pot. The milkman delivered the milk as usual, but when people took their milk indoors, they found the bottles were full of lemonade. Old Mr Smith tried to pull his chair up to the table and found it was stuck hard to the floor. And when Mrs Smith painted her bedroom blue, she came back and found it had changed to pink with purple spots.

Can you guess what had happened? Do you know who'd been up to all these tricks? It was an imp, of course! The wicked little fellow had become bored playing pranks on the fairies and goblins in fairyland. By now, they knew all his tricks and he was finding it harder and harder to catch them out. Then he had an idea. Why not play tricks in the human world where he would be invisible? So that's exactly what he did.

At first, he really only meant
to play one or two tricks, but he
had such fun that he couldn't
resist carrying on.

Well, the invisible imp continued
on with his tricks. But of course, as you know,
pride comes before a fall, and one day he just went too far. Sarah
Jones had been invited to a party. It was to be a fancy dress party
and on the invitation it said: "*Please wear red*". Now Sarah
fretted because she had no red clothes at all. Then she
had an idea. She got out an old blue frock from the
back of the cupboard. "I'll dye it red," she thought.

She mixed a big tub of red dye and was just about to put the
dress into it, when along came the invisible imp. "Here's some
fun!" he thought. "I'll turn the dye blue. Then she won't know
why her dress hasn't changed colour. Won't that be funny!" And
he started giggling to himself at the thought of it. He danced up
and down on the edge of the tub, thinking up
a really evil spell to turn the dye blue.
But he laughed so much to himself
that he slipped and fell right into
the bright red mixture. Fast as
lightning out he scrambled
and cast his spell.

28

Sure enough Sarah fished out the dress from the tub, and to her dismay saw that it was exactly the same colour as when she had put it into the dye. She was about to peer into the tub when something caught her eye. For there, sitting on the table, chuckling to himself and holding his sides with laughter, was a bright red imp. And there was a trail of tiny red footprints from the tub of dye to the table. The silly imp had no idea that he was no longer invisible and that Sarah could see him as plain as the nose on her face! In a flash Sarah realised what had happened. She chased the imp out of the house and down the street and, I'm glad to say, he wasn't able to play his mischievous tricks ever again.

29

# The Ugly Duckling

Once upon a time, there was a mother duck who laid a clutch of six beautiful little eggs. One day, she looked into her nest in amazement. For there were her six small eggs but lying next to them was another egg that was much, much bigger than the others. "That's odd," she thought, and went back to sitting on the nest.

Soon, one by one, the smaller eggs hatched, and out came six pretty yellow ducklings. Yet the bigger egg still had not hatched.

The mother duck sat on the large egg for another day and another night until eventually the egg cracked, and out tumbled a seventh duckling.

But this one was very different. He was big, with scruffy grey feathers and large brown feet.

"You do look different from my other chicks," exclaimed the mother duck, "but never mind, I'm sure you've got a heart of gold." And she cuddled him to her with all the other ducklings. Sure enough, he was very sweet-natured and happily played alongside the other ducklings.

One day, the mother duck led her ducklings down to the river to learn to swim. One by one they jumped into the water and splashed about. But when the big grey duckling leaped into the water he swam beautifully. He could swim faster and further than any of his brothers or sisters. The other ducklings were jealous and began to resent him.

"You're a big ugly duckling," they hissed at him. "You don't belong here." And when their mother wasn't looking they chased him right away.

The ugly duckling felt very sad as he waddled away across the fields. "I know I'm not fluffy and golden like my brothers and sisters," he said to himself. "I may have scruffy grey feathers and big brown feet, but I'm just as good as they are – and I'm better at swimming!" He sat down under a bush and started to cry. Just then he heard a terrible sound – CRACK! CRACK! It was the sound of a gun. There were men out there shooting ducks. Then, only a short way from where he was hiding, a dog rushed past him, sniffing the ground. The ugly duckling did not dare to move. He stayed under the bush until it was dark and only then did he feel it was safe to come out.

He set off, not knowing which way he was going until eventually, through the darkness, he saw a light shining. The light came from a cosy-looking cottage. The ugly duckling looked inside cautiously. He could see a fire burning in the hearth and sitting by the fire was an old woman with a hen and a cat.

"Come in, little duckling," said the old woman. "You are welcome to stay here. For now I can have duck's eggs each day as well as hen's eggs."

The ugly duckling was glad to warm himself by the fire. When the old lady had gone to bed, the hen and the cat cornered the duckling.

"Can you lay eggs?" enquired the hen.

"No," replied the duckling.

"Can you catch mice?" demanded the cat.

"No," replied the miserable duckling.

"Well, you're no use then, are you?" they sneered.

The next day, the old woman scolded the duckling: "You've been here a whole day and not one egg! You're no use, are you?"

So the ugly duckling waddled off out of the cottage. "I know when I'm not wanted," he said to himself mournfully.

He wandered along for a very long time until at last he reached a lake where he could live without anyone to bother him. He lived on the lake for many months. Gradually the days got shorter and the nights longer. The wind blew the leaves off the trees. Winter came and the weather turned bitterly cold. The lake froze over and the ugly duckling shivered under the reeds at the lake's edge. He was desperately cold, hungry and lonely, but he had nowhere else to go.

At last spring came, the weather got warmer and the ice on the lake melted. The ugly duckling felt the sun on his feathers. "I think I'll go for a swim," he thought. He swam right out into the middle of the lake, where the water was as clear as a mirror. He looked down at his reflection in the water and stared and stared. Staring back at him was a beautiful white bird with a long, elegant neck. "I'm no longer an ugly duckling," he said to himself, "but what am I?"

At that moment three big white birds just like himself flew towards him and landed on the lake. They swam right up to him and one of them said, "You are the handsomest swan that we have ever seen. Would you care to join us?"

"So *that's* what I am – I'm a swan," thought the bird that had been an ugly duckling. "I would love to join you," he said to the other swans. "Am I really a swan?" he asked, not quite believing it could be true.

"Of course you are!" replied the others. "Can't you see you're just like us?"

The three older swans became his best friends and the ugly duckling, that was now a beautiful swan, swam across the lake with them and there they lived together. He knew that he was one of them and that he would never be lonely again.

# The Mirror of Dreams

The house on the corner of Nightingale Avenue was tall and very handsome, and was by far the largest in the neighbourhood. From the street you could see four floors of beautifully decorated rooms, and if you peeped over the railings you could see the basement below. If you were lucky enough to be asked into the house, and passed through the beautiful hallways into the playroom, you might meet the owner's daughter, Cordelia. Sometimes Cordelia would be sitting in her silk pyjamas playing on her grand piano, and sometimes she would be dressed in the finest velvet gowns playing with her lovely dolls.

If you went down the stairs and into the basement, you might come across Polly. Polly's mother was a chambermaid in the house, and worked hard all day long to make the house sparkling clean. Sometimes Polly helped her to polish the ornaments and dust the furniture, but more often Polly sat on her own in her small bedroom drawing pictures with some crayons on a drawing pad she had been given for her birthday. When Polly was helping to polish the furniture she would look longingly at all of

Cordelia's fine clothes and toys, and when she sat alone in her room she would draw pictures of all the beautiful things she would like to own if only she could afford them.

One day, a large parcel was delivered to the house and taken upstairs to Cordelia's bedroom. A little while later, Cordelia's maid carried a pretty, ornate mirror down from her room and put it with the rubbish waiting for collection outside the house. Polly asked the maid why the mirror was to be thrown away, and the maid explained that Cordelia had been given a new mirror in which to brush her long, silky locks, and that she didn't need it any more. The maid then asked if Polly would like the old mirror, and of course Polly accepted with pleasure – it was the most beautiful thing she had ever owned.

Polly carried the mirror back to her room and polished it lovingly. As she polished the glass a strange thing started to happen. The glass went misty, and then cleared as her own reflection stared back at her once more. But the reflection that stared back was not dressed in rags and worn old clothes as Polly was, but in a rich gown of the most beautiful cream satin, with pink bows and apricot lace.

39

Polly was entranced. She looked almost as beautiful as Cordelia! Her hair gleamed and her fingers were white and magnificent. As she looked further into the mirror, she saw herself dancing at a ball, and then sitting down to eat the finest food she had ever seen – hams and roasted meats, and cakes of strawberries and cream!

And then the mirror spoke to her. "I am the Mirror of Dreams," the cool, clear voice said. "Whatever your heart desires most will be reflected in my shiny surface."

Polly was astounded, but so happy. She didn't care that it was only a day dream, for when she saw her reflection in the beautiful clothes, she felt as if she were truly there dancing and eating the fine foods – she could almost taste the fruit and cream in her mouth!

From that day on, Polly sat in her room every day, and dreamed and dreamed and dreamed. She had never felt so happy before, and could not wait to wake up each morning to visit her imaginary world. She certainly didn't understand how Cordelia could have thrown away such a magical wonder, and thought that she could not have known of its enchanting secret. She supposed also that Cordelia could have had no use for such a mirror, for whatever Cordelia wanted in real life she received, and would have no need to dream. But Polly was to find out that this was very far from true!

Weeks passed, and every day Polly sat and dreamed of ermine cloaks, of diamonds and pearls, of parties and picnics and carnivals. Eventually, she had dreamed every dream she had ever wanted. And Polly began to realise that it no longer made her as happy as it once had, and she began to grow weary of her Mirror of Dreams. She sat in front of the mirror less and less, and eventually when she did visit the mirror she could not think of a single thing that would make her happy. Even the dreams she had in which her mother wore fine silk clothes and didn't have to scrub and clean for their living could no longer make her happy.

She preferred her real mother, who came to kiss her good night and read her stories no matter how tired and overworked she was. Eventually she stopped looking in the mirror altogether, and finally decided to throw the mirror away – it had only made her more unhappy.

As the long winter turned into spring she acted upon her decision, and took down the mirror to throw away with the rubbish. But as she looked into the glass, it misted over in its familiar way and she saw herself in the mirror as she looked in real life, but in it she was playing with other children like herself, and reading stories with them and sharing toys. She felt gloriously happy, and knew in that instant that all she wanted was a very good friend. She realised in that moment, too, that perhaps Cordelia really had known the mirror's secret, but that she also had become more unhappy as the dreams faded and reality forced itself upon her. She wondered aloud what it was that Cordelia had dreamed of, and for the second and last time the mirror spoke in its cool, clear voice.

"The Mirror of Dreams showed Cordelia her heart's desire, and her heart desires a true friend and companion – someone who is not jealous of her wealth, but a friend who will share her hopes and dreams, and with whom she can have parties, games and picnics."

Polly put the mirror down and thought with amazement that she could be that friend, if Cordelia would be friends with someone poor but honest and true. Polly left the mirror with the household rubbish and was about to make the descent back to the basement, when she saw Cordelia standing in the garden at the back of the house. Cordelia had seen her discard the mirror, and shyly walked up to Polly. Polly overcame her shyness also and went to meet Cordelia, and then she told her they shared the same dream.

Cordelia and Polly became the best of friends from that day on. They shared everything they had, no matter how much or little. They talked and laughed together all day long, and they played long into the evening. They didn't have to dream any more, for they had both got their true heart's desire.

# The Bee Who Wanted More Stripes

Bertie the bee was a rather vain young bee. Every morning, as soon as he woke up, he would find a large dewdrop in which to admire his reflection. The thing that Bertie liked best about himself was his stripes. He thought stripes were the smartest, flashiest fashion accessory any animal could have. He just wished he had more stripes. But he only had a couple. "Still," he thought, "they are very fine stripes."

Then he had an idea. What if he could get some more stripes? He would be the stripiest bee around, and then everyone else would admire him, too. "I know what I'll do," he said. "I'll ask some other very stripy animals how they got all their stripes, and maybe I can copy them."

He buzzed off through the wood, looking for striped animals to ask. He flew across the fields and then the sea and at last he reached a place where there seemed to be quite a few striped animals. The first animal he approached looked like a striped horse. "Hello, Neddy!" said Bertie, landing on the beast's nose.

"I'm not a horse – I'm a zebra. And get off my nose!" said the zebra crossly.

"I do beg your pardon," said Bertie. "I just wanted to ask you how you got your stripes."

"Well," said the zebra, "I used to be all brown. Then one day I came across a piano in the middle of the plain. As I walked past the piano, its black and white keys started to play a tune all by themselves. Then I looked down and found I had turned black and white, too. And if you believe that you'll believe anything!" And with that the zebra laughed and trotted off.

Bertie continued on his way. Now he could see a large striped cat. "Hello, puss!" said Bertie, landing on the creature's back.

"I'm not a cat – I'm a tiger. And get off my back!" growled the tiger.

"I'm so sorry," said Bertie, "I just wanted to ask you how you got your stripes."

"Well," said the tiger, "I used to be all yellow. Then one day, when I was a cub, I was playing with a ball of black string and I got all tangled up in it. And that's how I got my stripes. And if you believe that you'll believe anything!"
And the tiger started to laugh
as he stalked off.

Bertie continued on his way. Soon he could see a long striped worm slithering through the grass. "Hello, little worm!" called Bertie, landing on the worm's tail.

"I'm not a worm – I'm a snake. And get off my tail!" hissed the snake.

"Oh dear. I didn't mean to upset you," said Bertie. "I just wanted to ask you how you got your stripes."

"Well," said the snake, "I used to be all brown. Then one day I was crossing a road just as the traffic lights were changing from red to green, and when I reached the other side I found that I was striped red and green from head to tail. And if you believe that you'll believe anything!" And the snake started to laugh as he slithered away.

Bertie continued on his way once more. Then he spotted a squirrel with a striped tail in a tree. "Hello, squirrel!" he said, landing on the animal's paw.

"I'm not a squirrel – I'm a ring-tailed lemur. And get off my paw!" said the ring-tailed lemur angrily.

"I do apologise," said Bertie. "I just wanted to ask you how you got your striped tail."

47

# Buried Treasure

Jim lived in a big old house with a big rambling garden. The house was rather spooky, and Jim much preferred the garden. He would spend hours kicking a football around the overgrown lawn, climbing the old apple trees in the orchard or just staring into the pond in case he might spot a fish. It was a wonderful garden to play in but Jim was not really a happy child because he was lonely. How he wished he had someone to play with! It would be such fun to play football with a friend, or have someone to go fishing with. He had plenty of friends at school, but it was a long bus journey to his home and besides, his school friends found his house so spooky that they only came to visit once.

One day Jim was hunting about in the garden with a stick. He hoped he might find some interesting small creatures to examine. Every time he found a new creature he would draw it and try to find out its name. So far, he had discovered eight types of snails and six different ladybirds. As he was poking about under some leaves he saw a piece of metal sticking out of the ground. He reached down and pulled it free. In his hand lay a rusty old key. It was quite big, and as Jim brushed away the soil, he saw that it was carved with beautiful patterns.

Jim carried the key indoors and cleaned it and polished it. Then he set about trying to find the lock that it fitted. First he tried the old garden gate that had been locked as long as Jim could remember. But the key was far too small. Next he tried the grandfather clock in the hall. But the key did not fit the clock's lock. Then he remembered an old wind-up teddy bear that played the drum. Jim hadn't played with the toy for a long time and he eagerly tried out the key, but this time it was too big.

51

The water felt deliciously warm and when he reached the shore
he found warm sand between his toes. He couldn't believe it! Here
he was on a desert island. The pirates went in all directions,
searching for something to make a shelter. Jim looked, too, and
under a rock he found a book. The book looked familiar to Jim.
He was sure he'd seen it somewhere before. He was still puzzling
over it when one of the pirates came running towards him waving
a knife. "You thief, you stole me rubies!" cursed the pirate in a
menacing voice. What was Jim to do?

Then he heard a voice call out from the book, "Quick! Step
into my pages." Without thinking twice, Jim stepped into the
book and suddenly he was back in the attic again.

Jim peered closely at the page from which he'd just stepped. *The Pirates and the Stolen Treasure* it said at the top of the page. Jim read the page and found he was reading exactly the adventure he had been in. He turned excitedly to the contents page at the front of the book and read the chapter titles. *Journey to Mars*, he read, and *The Castle Under the Sea*. Further down it said: *The Magic Car* and *Into the Jungle*. Jim was thrilled. He realised that he could open the book at any page and become part of the adventure, and he only had to find the book and step into it to get back to the attic again.

After that, Jim had many, many adventures. He made lots of friends in the stories and he had lots of narrow escapes. But he always found the book again just in time. Jim was never lonely again.

# Goldilocks and the Three Bears

There once lived a little girl who had long, golden hair. Because of this, everyone knew her as Goldilocks. Goldilocks and her mother lived together in a cosy little cottage in the forest.

"Would you like some pretty flowers?" Goldilocks asked her mother one day. "I will pick you some if you like."

"That would be lovely, my dear," said her mother. "But mind you don't get lost. Don't stray too far, and don't be too long."

Goldilocks gave her mother a big hug and promised to be careful. She picked up her little flower basket and skipped off into the forest to look for flowers.

First she came upon some big, bright daffodils. She picked a few and placed them in her basket. A little further on, she spied some pretty bluebells and so she picked a bunch of those as well. Then she saw, even further on, some lovely marigolds which she also picked and put into her basket.

Well, Goldilocks was so busy picking all these wonderful flowers that she wandered further and further into the forest. Suddenly she realised that she was lost. She didn't know which way to turn. She was also beginning to feel very hungry and tired.

Just when she was wondering what to do next, she saw a small cottage nestling among the trees. She went up to it and looked through the windows, but couldn't see anyone inside. But the door was open and so she went in. Inside the cottage she found a table laid out with three bowls of steaming porridge. There was a big bowl, a medium-sized bowl and a little bowl. The table also had three chairs arranged around it, one next to each of the bowls of porridge. There was a big chair, a medium-sized chair and a little chair.

Goldilocks was so tired that she simply had to sit down. First she sat down in the big chair, but it was very hard and lumpy. It wasn't comfortable at all. Then she tried the medium-sized chair, but that didn't feel comfortable either. At last, she tried the little chair, but as soon as she sat down in it – it broke! She was too heavy for the little chair. "Oh dear," thought Goldilocks.

Instead of sitting down, she thought she would have some porridge as she was still very hungry. First she took a spoonful of porridge from the big bowl. But it was too hot, and so she couldn't eat it. Then she tried a spoonful from the medium-sized bowl, but it was too lumpy. So she tried a spoonful from the little bowl. And guess what? It tasted so delicious that she ate it all up!

"Oh, I do feel sleepy," yawned Goldilocks after she had finished the porridge in the little bowl. "I wonder if there is a nice, comfortable bed I can sleep in."

So she went upstairs and found a bedroom with three beds in it. There was a big bed, a medium-sized bed and a little bed. First she tried the big bed, but it was very hard and didn't feel comfortable at all. Next she tried the medium-sized bed, but it was too soft and that didn't feel comfortable either. Finally, she tried the little bed. It was just right – warm and cosy. Soon she was fast asleep.

Just then, the family of three bears who lived in the cottage came back from their walk in the forest. As soon as they came in through the front door, they knew someone had been there.

60

"Who has been sitting in
my chair?" said Daddy Bear,
in a deep, gruff voice.

"And who has been
sitting in my chair?"
asked Mummy Bear
in a softer voice.

"Who has broken
my chair?" cried Baby
Bear in a squeaky voice.

Then the three bears looked on the table.

"Someone has been trying my porridge," said Daddy Bear.

"And someone has been trying my porridge, too," said Mummy Bear.

"Who has eaten all my porridge?" said Baby Bear, who by now was very upset and sobbing big tears.

Upstairs went the three bears and into their bedroom.

"Who has been sleeping in my bed?" asked Daddy Bear.

"And who has been sleeping in my bed?" asked Mummy Bear.

Suddenly, Baby Bear gave a cry of surprise. "Look!" he yelled.

"There's someone sleeping in my bed."

Goldilocks woke up with a start when she heard all the noise. She looked up to see the three bears staring down at her. She was so frightened that she jumped straight out of bed, down the stairs and out through the front door. Then she ran and ran until she arrived back home to her own cottage again.

And do you know, that was the last that the three bears ever saw of Goldilocks!

# The Chocolate Soldier

In the window of Mrs Brown's sweet shop there stood a chocolate soldier. He had chocolate ears, chocolate eyebrows and a curly chocolate moustache of which he was particularly proud. But best of all he loved his shiny foil uniform with its braid on the shoulders and cuffs, and smart red stripes down each leg. All day long the chocolate soldier stood to attention on a shelf in the window, staring straight ahead out into the street. Standing next to him on the shelf were more chocolate soldiers, and beyond them he could see some sugar mice and a twist of liquorice bootlaces.

It was summer time and the sun shone through the window of the sweet shop. At first the chocolate soldier felt pleasantly warm; then he started to feel uncomfortably hot. Next he began to feel most peculiar indeed. His chocolate moustache was wilting and his arms were dripping. Soon he was completely melted and before he knew it, he had slipped out through a hole in his silver foil shoe and was pouring off the shelf and out into the street.

Down the street he poured.

"Stop! Help!" he shouted, but nobody heard his cries. Now he could hear the sound of gushing water and, to his horror, he could see he was heading for a stream at the bottom of the street.

"Help me! I can't swim! I'm going to drown!" the chocolate soldier cried as he plunged into the cold, running water. But now something very strange was happening. He found he could swim quite easily. He looked round and saw that he had a chocolate tail covered in scales. He looked down at his arms, but there was a pair of fins instead. The cold water had hardened him into the shape of a chocolate fish!

The chocolate soldier was carried downstream, and after a while the stream broadened out and became a river. He realised that he would soon be carried out to sea.

65

"Whatever shall I do?" wondered the chocolate soldier. "I'm sure to get eaten by a bigger fish or maybe even a shark!" He tried to turn around and swim against the river's flow but it was no good. The current swept him away down river again.

Soon he could see the waves on the shore. He smelt the sea air and tasted the salt in the water. Now he found himself bobbing up and down on the sea. He could see a boat not far away and then all of a sudden he felt a net closing around him. He struggled to get out, but the net only tightened and soon he felt himself being hauled out of the water and landed with a "thwack!" on the deck among a pile of fish. The smell was awful, and the chocolate soldier was quite relieved when he felt the boat being rowed towards the shore.

"I'll hop over the side as soon as we land and run away," he thought, quite forgetting that he had no legs but only a fish's tail.

But there was no chance of escape. As soon as the boat reached the shore, he and all the other fish were flung into buckets and lifted into a van. The van stopped outside a shop and a man carried the buckets inside, where it smelt of fried fish, chips and vinegar. The chocolate soldier found himself being lifted up with a lot of other fish in a huge metal basket. He looked down and saw a terrible sight below. They were heading for a vat of boiling oil! At that very moment he felt very peculiar once again. His scales melted, his tail drooped and he felt himself slide through the holes in the basket and into the pocket of a man's overalls.

The chocolate soldier lay in the corner of the pocket, while the man worked all day in the shop. Then the man headed for home, with the chocolate soldier bouncing up and down in the overall pocket as the man walked along. Soon they arrived at the man's house. He reached into his pocket.

"Look what I've found," he said to his small son. "A coin. Here, you can have it – but don't spend it all at once!" he said, chuckling to himself. The chocolate soldier felt himself being passed from one hand to another.

"So now I've hardened into the shape of a chocolate coin," he thought. "And I'm going to be eaten by the boy!" But to his surprise he found himself being slipped into the boy's pocket.

The chocolate soldier felt himself bouncing up and down in the child's pocket as he ran up the street and into a shop. The chocolate soldier peeped out and to his astonishment saw that he was back in Mrs Brown's sweet shop. Then he realised what was happening. The boy believed he was a real coin and was going to try and spend him! The boy stood in the queue at the counter.

The chocolate soldier called out to his soldier friends in the window, "Pssst! It's me! Help me get out of here!" One of the soldiers looked down, but all he could see was a chocolate coin sticking out of the boy's pocket. Then he recognised the voice.

"I'm a chocolate soldier like you, but I've been turned into a coin. Help!" cried the chocolate soldier.

"Leave it to me," replied the soldier on the shelf. "Don't worry, we'll have you out of there in a jiffy!"

The word was passed along and, quick as a flash, one of the sugar mice chewed off a length of liquorice bootlace. Then the soldier lowered the lace into the boy's pocket, where it stuck to the chocolate coin. Carefully the soldiers hauled the coin up on to the shelf. The chocolate soldier was delighted to find his foil uniform was still there on the shelf, just where it had been before. All the effort of getting on to the shelf had made him quite warm, and he found he could slip quite easily back through the hole in the shoe and into his uniform again.

"I'd like a chocolate soldier," said the boy to Mrs Brown. But when he reached in his pocket the coin had gone.

"Never mind," said kind Mrs Brown, "I'll let you have one anyway." She reached into the window and took down a soldier from the end of the row and gave it to the boy. And as for our chocolate soldier? In the cool of the night he turned back into a smart-looking soldier again.

69

# Peter Meets a Dragon

Once upon a time there was a young boy named Peter. He lived in an ordinary house with an ordinary Mum and Dad, an ordinary sister and an ordinary pet cat, called Jasper. In fact, everything in Peter's life was so ordinary that he sometimes wished that something extraordinary would happen. "Why doesn't a giant come and squash the house flat with his foot?" he wondered, and "If only a pirate would take my sister hostage!" But each day, Peter would wake up in the morning and everything was just the same as it had been the day before.

One morning Peter woke up to find a very strange smell in the house. Looking out of his bedroom window, he saw that the front lawn was scorched and blackened. There was smoke drifting off the grass and, further away, he could see some bushes ablaze.

Peter rushed downstairs and out of the front door. He ran out of the garden and down the lane following the trail of smoke and burning grass. He grew more and more puzzled, however, as there was no sign of anything that could have caused such a blaze.

Peter was about to run home and tell his Mum and Dad, when he heard a panting noise coming from the undergrowth. Parting the bushes gently with his hands he found a young creature. It had green, scaly skin, a pair of wings and a long snout full of sharp teeth. Every now and again a little tongue of flame came from its nostrils, setting the grass around it on fire. "A baby dragon!" Peter said to himself, in great surprise. Big tears were rolling out of the dragon's yellow eyes and down its scaly cheeks as it flapped its wings desperately and tried to take off.

When the dragon saw Peter it stopped flapping its wings. "Oh, woe is me!" it sobbed. "Where am I?"

"Where do you want to be?" asked Peter, kneeling down on the scorched ground.

71

"I want to be in Dragonland with my friends," replied the dragon. "We were all flying together, but I just couldn't keep up with them. I got tired and needed a rest. I called to the others but they didn't hear me. Then I just had to stop and get my breath back. Now I don't know where I am, or if I'll ever see my friends again!" And with that the baby dragon started to cry once more.

"I'm sure I can help. I'll get you home," said Peter, though he had no idea how.

"You?" hissed a voice nearby. "How could you possibly help? You're just a boy!" Peter looked round, and to his astonishment found Jasper sitting behind him. "I suppose you're going to wave a magic wand, are you?" continued Jasper. "You need to call in an expert." Then he turned his back on Peter and the baby dragon and started washing his paws.

Peter was astounded. He'd never heard Jasper talking before. He had thought he was just an ordinary pet cat. "W… w… what do you mean?" he stammered.

"Well," said Jasper, glancing over his shoulder at Peter, "I reckon that horse over there could help. Follow me."

So Peter and the baby dragon – whose name was Flame – followed Jasper over to where the horse stood at the edge of a field. Jasper leaped up on to the gate and called to the horse. Then he whispered in the horse's ear. The horse thought for a moment, then whispered back in Jasper's ear. "He says he's got a friend on the other side of the wood who'll help," said Jasper.

"But how?" said Peter, looking perplexed.

"Be patient! Follow me!" said Jasper as he stalked off through the grass. "And tell your friend to stop setting fire to everything!" he added. Peter saw, to his horror, that Flame was indeed blazing a trail through the field.

"I can't help it," cried Flame, about to burst into tears again. "Every time I get out of breath I start to pant, and then I start breathing fire."

"Let me carry you," said Peter. He picked Flame up in his arms and ran after Jasper. The baby dragon felt very strange. His body was all cold and clammy, but his mouth was still breathing hot smoke, which made Peter's eyes water.

He ran through the wood, just keeping Jasper's upright tail in sight. On the other side of the wood was another field, and in the field was a horse. But this was no ordinary horse. Peter stopped dead in his tracks and stared. The horse was pure milky white, and from its head grew a single, long horn. "A unicorn!" breathed Peter.

Jasper was already talking to the unicorn. He beckoned with his paw to Peter. "He'll take your friend home and you can go, too, Peter, but don't be late for tea, or you know what your mother will say." And with that, Jasper was off.

"Climb aboard," said the unicorn gently.

Peter and the little dragon scrambled up on to the unicorn's back. "What an adventure," thought Peter. Up, up, and away they soared through the clouds.

Flame held tightly on to Peter's hand with his clammy paw. At last Peter could see a mountain ahead through the clouds. Now they were descending through the clouds again, and soon the unicorn landed right at the top of the mountain. "I'm home!" squeaked Flame joyously as they landed. Sure enough, several dragons were running over to greet him. They looked quite friendly, but some of them were rather large and one was breathing a great deal of fire.

"Time for me to go," said Peter a little nervously, as Flame jumped off the unicorn's back and flew to the ground. The unicorn took off again and soon they were back in the field once more.

As he slid off the unicorn's back, Peter turned to thank him, but when he looked he saw that it was just an ordinary horse with no trace of a horn at all. Peter walked back home across the field, but there was no sign of burnt grass. He reached his own front lawn, which was also in perfect condition. Peter felt more and more perplexed. "I hope Jasper can explain," he thought, as the cat ran past him and into the house. "Jasper, I took the baby dragon home. What's happened to the burnt grass?" he blurted out. But Jasper said not a word. He ignored Peter and curled up in his basket.

When Peter wasn't looking, however, Jasper gave him a glance that seemed to say, "Well, was that a big enough adventure for you?"

# Ursula's Umbrella

Ursula was a little girl who longed for adventure. She loved reading stories about far-away places and explorers, and even children like herself who had amazing adventures. "Why doesn't anything interesting ever happen to me?" she sighed. "How I wish I could fly to the moon or dive to the deepest part of the ocean. What fun it would be!"

One windy day, Ursula went out for a walk. She took her umbrella with her because it looked as though it might be going to rain. Ursula's umbrella was red with a shiny black handle. It was also very large indeed. People used to laugh as Ursula walked along the street with her umbrella up. It looked so big and Ursula was so small that it seemed as though the umbrella was walking along all by itself!

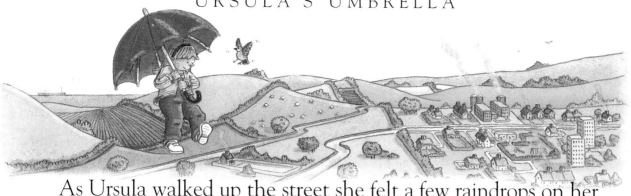

As Ursula walked up the street she felt a few raindrops on her nose. "Better put up my umbrella," she thought. She unfurled her umbrella and lifted it up above her head. As she did so, a great gust of wind came and swept her right off the pavement. It carried her past the upstairs windows of the houses, past the roofs and the chimney pots and up, up, into the sky. Ursula clung tightly to the umbrella handle. She was surprised to find she didn't feel the least bit frightened. No, not a bit. She felt very excited. She looked down and saw streets and factories whizzing past far below. Then she saw fields and something that looked like a silver thread snaking through the countryside. "A river!" thought Ursula.

Now she could see the coastline, and soon the umbrella was carrying her out over the ocean. At first when she looked down the sea was grey, but gradually it turned to the deepest blue with frothy white waves. "How I'd love a swim," thought Ursula. At that moment she felt the umbrella starting to descend. Looking down she could see that they were heading for an island in the middle of the ocean. Soon she was floating past the tops of palm trees and, as she touched the ground, she felt sand under her feet.

"I'm going for a swim!" said Ursula to herself. She folded up her umbrella and set off to the beach. The water felt deliciously warm as Ursula paddled about. She looked down and saw that the water was amazingly clear. She could see brightly coloured fish darting in and out of the coral. "Wow!" exclaimed Ursula out loud and then "Wow!" again, though this time much louder as she looked up and saw a black fin skimming through the water towards her. "Shark!" she shrieked, but no-one heard.

Then all of a sudden a gust of wind made her umbrella unfurl itself and float towards her in the water, like a boat. Ursula made a dash for the umbrella, hurled herself into it and floated away across the sea. "That was quite an adventure!" she thought.

After a while, Ursula looked out over the rim of the umbrella and saw that it was heading for the shore again. This time, when Ursula stepped out of the umbrella, she found that she was at the edge of a jungle. Folding up the umbrella, she set off into the forest. She followed an overgrown path through the trees. "I wonder where this leads?" thought Ursula. She wiped her brow and swatted the insects that flew in front of her face. Deeper and deeper into the jungle she went.

Suddenly she heard the sound of rushing water and found herself standing on the banks of a river. All at once she heard another sound. It was the crashing noise of some enormous beast approaching through the trees:

79

Where could she run to? Suddenly she felt the umbrella being blown from her hand. To her amazement it fell to the ground, stretching right across the river like a bridge. Ursula walked over to the other side, not daring to look down at the torrent below. When she was safely on the far bank she looked back to see a large puma, with glittering green eyes, glaring at her from the opposite bank. "That was a lucky escape!" thought Ursula.

Ursula could see a mountain through the trees and decided to head towards it. "I'll be able to get a good view from the top and maybe find my way home," she thought. She struggled on through the forest and eventually found herself at the foot of the mountain. There seemed to be no way up the sheer rock face.

Ursula was on the point of despair when suddenly another great gust of wind blew up. It carried Ursula, clinging to her opened umbrella, all the way up to the top of the mountain.

# URSULA'S UMBRELLA

At the top of the mountain, the umbrella let her gently down again and her feet landed in deep snow. By now it was blowing a blizzard and she could not see anything except white snowflakes in all directions. "There's only one thing to do," thought Ursula. She put the umbrella on the snow, sat on it and whizzed all the way down the other side of the mountain.

When she reached the bottom, to her surprise, the umbrella sledge didn't stop but carried on through the snowstorm until eventually, after a very long time, it came to a halt right outside her own front door. "Well, that was quite an adventure," said Ursula, shaking the snow off the umbrella, before folding it up.

She stepped inside the front door. "Wherever have you been?" said her mother. "You look as though you've been to the ends of the Earth and back."

"Well I have," Ursula was about to say. But then she thought that no-one would believe her and it was nicer to keep her adventures to herself. And that is what she did.

# Cinderella

Once upon a time there was a beautiful young girl who lived with her widowed father. He had brought her up to be kind and gentle. All went well until the day the girl's father married again. His second wife was very proud of her house. Everything always had to be spotlessly clean. Worse than that, she had two spiteful daughters. All three had terrible tempers, and they hated the beautiful young girl with a vengeance. All day long from dawn to dusk she was made to scrub and clean, mend clothes and serve at the table. At night, while the household slept, there was coal to fetch, fires to be laid and the table to be set for breakfast the following day.

The stepmother gave her own two daughters the finest rooms in the house. To her stepdaughter, she gave the coldest attic room, with the hardest bed and a quilt cover that was so thin it barely kept out the winter chill. To keep warm, the poor girl had to sit in the chimney nook of the kitchen with her feet near the cinders. Because of this, her stepsisters nicknamed her Cinderella.

One day a footman called at the house to deliver an invitation. Cinderella carried it into the dining room where her stepsisters were having breakfast. "What have you there?" shrieked one of them, snatching the envelope from her hand. She tore it open with her long, polished nails. "Ooh!" she cried. "It's an invitation from the prince to attend a ball tomorrow night!"

The other sister jumped up and down with delight. "We're going to a ball!" she yelled.

"Am I invited, too?" asked Cinderella shyly.

"You?" cried the elder sister.

"You – invited to the palace ball?" cried the other sister, and they both burst into fits of laughter. The elder sister, who was very plump, laughed so much that she became quite breathless and had to ask Cinderella to loosen her corset.

The sisters spent the next day preparing for the ball. Cinderella was kept very busy, pressing and starching the girls' ballgowns, curling their hair and fixing bows and ribbons. They told her to lace their corsets extra tight to make them look slimmer. She was made to run hither and thither all day. "Fetch my pearl necklace!" called one.

"Polish my party shoes!" demanded the other. At last both sisters were ready to go, and set off by carriage to the ball. "Don't wait up!" they shouted out of the window to Cinderella, as the coach sped away.

Cinderella went back into the kitchen. Now the house seemed calm and quiet at last. She picked up a broom and danced slowly round the room, imagining that she was at the ball. "How wonderful it would be to go to the ball," she sighed wistfully, and sat down by the fire where it was warm and started to cry.

"Don't cry, my child," said a gentle voice.

Cinderella looked up to see a beautiful stranger standing before her. "Who are you?" said Cinderella.

"I am your fairy godmother," came the reply. "Now, dry your tears. Would you like to go to the ball?" said the fairy.

"Oh, yes please," cried Cinderella, leaping up.

"Then you shall go," said the fairy. "But first, run into the garden, and fetch me a nice fat pumpkin." Cinderella did as she was told. When she returned, the fairy godmother tapped the pumpkin with her magic wand and instantly it was transformed into a sparkling glass coach.

"Now we need some horses," said the fairy. At that moment there was a scuttling noise in the corner of the kitchen and four white mice popped out of a hole. In an instant the fairy godmother tapped them with her wand and they became four handsome white horses. "Now what about a footman," she said. Before Cinderella could speak she tapped Cinderella's black cat and there before her very eyes stood a footman. "Now there's just one more thing we need before you go," said the fairy, "and that's a coachman."

Cinderella looked about the kitchen and scratched her head.

85

Then she ran into the garden and came back with a live frog. "Will he do?" she asked her fairy godmother.

"Indeed he will," replied the fairy, tapping the frog. And suddenly there was a coachman standing by the coach.

"All aboard!" he cried.

Cinderella was just about to leap inside when her godmother called her back. "I nearly forgot something," she said.

The tip of her wand touched Cinderella's ragged clothes, and Cinderella looked down to see, to her astonishment, that she was wearing the most beautiful ballgown that there ever was. At her neck glittered a diamond necklace and on her feet were a dainty pair of glass slippers. "Have a lovely time at the ball," said her godmother. "But do not stay a minute longer than midnight, for on the stroke of twelve, everything will be as it was before."

And with that, she vanished.

When Cinderella arrived at the ball, she found herself in a dazzling ballroom filled with people. Everyone stopped to stare at this beautiful girl, and soon the prince himself approached and asked her to dance. "Who is she?" people were asking. The prince and Cinderella danced together all evening. Her stepsisters watched, never once guessing who she was.

"Isn't she beautiful," remarked the elder sister jealously.

"Such a tiny waist – she might snap in two!" whispered the other spitefully, and they both roared with laughter.

When the banquet was served the prince insisted that Cinderella sit next to him, and after dinner they danced again. Cinderella was enjoying herself so much she forgot all about the time. It was only when the clock struck midnight that she remembered her godmother's warning. She fled from the ballroom without a backward glance. The prince hurried after her but she ran faster than he. As she sped down the steps her ballgown turned to rags and she dropped one of her glass slippers. The prince picked it up. By the time she reached home, Cinderella was exhausted.

Soon her sisters arrived home. "There was the most beautiful princess at the ball," said one.

"The prince fell in love with her, and he was deeply saddened when she left at midnight," said the other.

As for the prince, he spent all night with the glass slipper pressed to his cheek, mourning the loss of the most wonderful girl he had ever set eyes upon. The next morning he was determined to find her. He sent his servant to all corners of the kingdom. "I will marry the girl whose foot fits the slipper," he declared. Well, every princess, duchess and lady in the land tried on the slipper, but none of them could fit the tiny shoe on her foot.

At last the servant called at the house of Cinderella and her stepsisters. "Me first!" they cried, pushing each other out of the way. One sister tried on the slipper but her toes were so fat that she couldn't squeeze them into the dainty shoe. Then the other sister tried, but her toes were so long they wouldn't fit either.

Cinderella had been watching from her corner by the fire. Now she came forward. "May I try on the shoe?" she asked timidly.

The stepsisters shrieked, "Don't be absurd! You weren't even at the ball."

But the prince's servant said, "If you wish to try on the slipper, then you shall." Cinderella slid her foot into the glass slipper and of course it fitted perfectly. The stepsisters were completely speechless with rage.

At that moment there was a flash of bright light and Cinderella's fairy godmother appeared. She touched Cinderella with her magic wand and immediately the girl's rags were transformed into the ballgown that she had worn the night before. Then her sisters recognised the beautiful princess they had seen at the ball. They fell upon their knees and begged forgiveness for the way they had treated her, hoping that they, too, might be invited to the palace. The servant escorted Cinderella to the palace and when the prince saw her, he immediately asked her to marry him. At the wedding there was much rejoicing and the sisters were so well behaved that they, too, received marriage proposals and they all lived happily ever after.

# Catswhiskers

Catswhiskers was a pyjama case cat, and a very fine-looking pyjama case cat at that. Susie's granny had sewn him together when Susie was only four years old. It had taken Susie's granny quite a long time to make Catswhiskers. Every night she had sat by the fire carefully cutting and sewing, until he was perfect. Catswhiskers' body was made from the finest black velvet. He had beautiful red glass eyes, a bushy tail and the longest whiskers you have ever seen. That is how he got the name Catswhiskers. Catswhiskers sat on the end of Susie's bed, looking at all the toys in the bedroom in that slightly snooty way that cats have of looking at things.

When Susie was asleep, or playing in another room, Catswhiskers and all the toys would talk to each other. But Catswhiskers was bored with talking to the toys. Jenny the ragdoll was – well – just a ragdoll. "What could a ragdoll possibly have to say that would be of interest to a velvet pyjama case cat?" thought Catswhiskers.

Then there was Neddy the rocking horse. He was a perfectly pleasant rocking horse as far as rocking horses went, but he only ever seemed to want to talk about how nice and shiny he was, and how he thought he was Susie's favourite toy. Even the alphabet bricks, the jack-in-the-box and the brightly coloured ball seemed to have nothing to say of interest to Catswhiskers. He sighed and looked at the window, wondering if life was more exciting outside.

One day, he decided he'd had enough of life in the bedroom with all the toys, and that he would venture outside to see if he could meet someone more interesting to talk to. So that night, when it was dark and Susie was asleep, he crept carefully to the open bedroom window and jumped out. It was a clear, cold, moonlit night. Catswhiskers shivered a little to find it so cold outside, and he maybe shivered a little more because he was also rather frightened. But he was very excited to be in the outside world, too, and he soon forgot about the cold and his fear.

He walked along the fence to the end of Susie's garden and jumped down into the garden next door. He had no sooner landed when he heard a fierce growl and saw two big, black eyes glinting in the moonlight.

It was Barker, next door's dog – and he didn't like cats at all. With a loud bark, Barker came rushing towards Catswhiskers. His mouth was open wide and Catswhiskers could see his big, sharp teeth. In fact, he thought that he could see all the way down into Barker's stomach! Catswhiskers only just had time to leap back on to the fence as Barker, jaws still snapping, gave chase.

"Phew, what a narrow escape," gasped Catswhiskers. "I didn't realise dogs were so unfriendly!"

He was wondering where it might be safe to go next when he heard a low, hissing voice behind him. "Hey, velvet cat," hissed the voice. "What do you think you are doing on *our* patch?"

Catswhiskers turned round to see the biggest, meanest-looking cat he had ever set eyes on. And behind *him* were several more mean-looking cats, all coming slowly towards Catswhiskers with their sharp claws at the ready. Catswhiskers didn't wait a second longer. He simply ran for his life.

Now he was very frightened. He was also feeling cold and hungry. He wished that he was still in the warm safety of Susie's bedroom with the other toys. Just as he was thinking that the outside world was perhaps a bit *too* exciting, he heard the sound of a van approaching. It suddenly stopped, its glaring headlights shining straight at him. On the side of the van were the words STRAY CAT CATCHER.

Out of the van stepped a man carrying a big net.
Catswhiskers thought he knew just who that net was for, and
decided that it was definitely time to go!

Without thinking about the dangers he might find himself in
if he came face to face again with gangs of sharp-clawed cats or
fierce, barking dogs, he ran back towards Susie's house as fast as
his velvet legs could carry him. At last he reached the window
and jumped thankfully back inside.

Snuggled down again on the warm bed with all his familiar
friends around him, Catswhiskers decided that perhaps this was
the best life for a pyjama case cat after all.

# The Castle in the Clouds

There was once a family that lived in a little house in a village at the bottom of a mountain. At the top of the mountain was a great, grey castle made of granite. The castle was always shrouded in clouds, so it was known as the castle in the clouds. From the village you could only just see the outline of its high walls and turrets. No-one in the village ever went near the castle, for it looked such a gloomy and forbidding place.

Now in this family there were seven children. One by one they went out into the world to seek their fortune, and at last it was the youngest child's turn. His name was Sam. His only possession was a pet cat named Jess, and she was an excellent rat-catcher. Sam was most upset at the thought of leaving Jess behind when he went off to find work, but then he had an idea.

"I'll offer Jess's services at the castle in the clouds. They're bound to need a good ratter, and I'm sure I can find work there, too," he thought.

His parents were dismayed to discover that Sam intended to seek work at the castle, but try as they might they could not change his mind. So Sam set off for the castle with Jess at his side. Soon the road started to wind up the mountainside through thick pine forests. It grew cold and misty. Rounding a bend they suddenly found themselves up against a massive, grey stone wall. They followed the curve of the wall until they came to the castle door.

Sam went up to the door and banged on it. The sound echoed spookily. "Who goes there?" said a voice.

Looking up, Sam saw that a window high in the wall had been thrown open and a face was eyeing him suspiciously.

97

"I... I... I wondered if you'd be interested in employing my cat as a rat-catcher," began Sam.

The window slammed shut, but a moment later a hand beckoned him through the partly open castle door. Stepping inside, Sam and Jess found themselves face-to-face with an old man. "Rat-catcher, did you say?" said the old man raising one eyebrow. "Very well, but she'd better do a good job or my master will punish us all!"

Sam sent Jess off to prove her worth. In the meantime Sam asked the old man, who was the castle guard, if there might be any work for him, too.

"You can help out in the kitchens. It's hard work, mind!" the guard said.

Sam was soon at work in the kitchens – and what hard work it was! He spent all day peeling vegetables, cleaning pans and scrubbing the floor. By midnight he was exhausted. He was about to find a patch of straw to make his bed, when he noticed Jess wasn't around. He set off in search of her. Down dark passages he went, up winding staircases, looking in every corner and behind every door, but there was no sign of her. By now he was hopelessly lost and was wondering how he would ever find his way back to the kitchens, when he caught sight of Jess's green eyes shining like lanterns at the top of a rickety spiral staircase. "Here, Jess!" called Sam softly. But Jess stayed just where she was.

When he reached her, he found that she was sitting outside a door and seemed to be listening to something on the other side. Sam put his ear to the door. He could hear the sound of sobbing. He knocked gently at the door. "Who is it?" said a girl's voice.

"I'm Sam, the kitchen boy. What's the matter? Can I come in?" said Sam.

"If only you could," sobbed the voice. "I'm Princess Rose. When my father died my uncle locked me in here so that he could steal the castle. Now I fear I shall never escape!"

Sam pushed and pushed at the door, but to no avail. "Don't worry," he said, "I'll get you out of here."

99

# The Greedy Hamster

There was once a hamster named Harry. He was a very greedy hamster. As soon as his food was put in his cage he gobbled it all up, and then he would push his little nose through the bars in the hope that something else to eat might come within reach. From his cage he could see all manner of delicious food on the kitchen table – and the smells! The scent of freshly baked bread was enough to send him spinning round in his exercise wheel with frustration.

"It's not fair!" he grumbled to himself. "They're all eating themselves silly out there and here am I simply starving to death!" (At this point he would usually remember the large meal he had just eaten and that his tummy was indeed still rather full.)

"If only I could get out of this beastly cage, I could feast on all the food I deserve," he announced to himself, and the thought of all those tasty morsels made his mouth water.

One night after the family had gone to bed, Harry was having one last spin in his wheel before retiring to his sawdust mattress. As he spun around, he heard an unfamiliar squeaky noise.

"That's funny," thought Harry. "The little girl oiled my wheel only today. It surely can't need oiling again." He stopped running and got off the wheel, but the squeak continued. Harry sat quite still on his haunches and listened intently. Then he realised it was the door to his cage squeaking. The door! The door was flapping open. The little girl had not closed it properly before she went to bed. Harry did a little dance of glee. Then he went to the door and looked cautiously out in case there was any danger. But all seemed to be well. The cat was asleep on a chair. The dog was sleeping soundly on the floor.

"Of course, I'd be only too pleased to help," said the crafty cat, thinking to herself here was an extra dinner! With her strong claws she bent back the door frame of the cage, until there was just enough room for Harry to squeeze through. Then, with a mighty swipe of her paw, she caught him and gobbled him whole. She felt extremely full, what with Harry and all his food inside her. She could barely crawl back to her chair and soon she was fast asleep again and snoring loudly with her mouth open. Inside her tummy Harry, too, felt very uncomfortable. Every time the cat snored, it sounded like a thunderstorm raging around his head.

"I must get out of here," he thought, and headed for the cat's open jaws. But he was far too fat to get out again. Then he had another idea. Through the cat's jaws he could see the dog lying on the floor.

"Help! Help!" he squeaked. The dog woke up to a very strange sight. There was the cat lying on the chair snoring, but she also seemed to be squeaking, "Help!" The dog put his head on one side. He was very perplexed. Then he saw a pair of beady eyes and some fine whiskers inside the cat's mouth. It was Harry!

"Get me out of here, please," pleaded Harry.

Now the dog did not very much like the cat, so he was quite willing to help the hamster.

"I'll stick my tail in the cat's mouth. Then you hang on while I pull you out," said the dog. "But mind you don't make a sound and wake the cat, or she'll surely bite my tail!" The dog gingerly put the tip of his tail inside the cat's open jaws, just far enough for Harry's little paws to grab hold. Then he pulled with all his might. Out popped Harry and out of Harry popped all the food he'd stored in his cheeks – peanuts, an apple core and a slice of jam tart!

"Thank you,  thank you," gasped Harry as he made a dash for his cage and slammed the door shut. "I think I'll stay in my cage from now on and just stick to the food I'm given!"

# The Three Little Pigs

Once upon a time there were three little pigs who lived on a farm with their mother and father. They decided that, although they were just little pigs, they were quite grown up enough to make their way in the big wide world, so one day they set off together to make their fortunes.

After they had walked for quite some time, one of the little pigs started to feel rather tired. Just then, a farmer went by on his haycart.

"Hey, stop cart," the first little pig yelled. "You stronger brothers go on without me," he said. "This hay is light enough and soft enough for my house." And with that his brothers left the little pig with his pile of hay, and carried on their journey.

A little further down the road, the second little pig grew very tired. Just then, they passed by a forester cutting wood.

"Would you sell me some of your wood?" asked the second little pig. "This wood isn't too heavy and it isn't too rough for my house – it's just right." And with that the third little pig carried on his journey. Soon, even the third little pig grew very tired, and up ahead he spotted a builder making a wall out of stone.

"Aha," he thought, "that's exactly what I need to build my house, as it's strong and tough, just like me." And so he bought some stone and built himself a house.

That evening, just as the first little pig was settling comfortably in his bed of hay, he heard a rustling outside the house. He easily parted the hay with his hands to look outside, and gulped in fright when he saw the big bad wolf looking at him greedily.

"Little piggy, little piggy, will you let me in?"

"Not on the hairs of my chinny chin chin, I will not let you in," shuddered the first little pig.

"Then I'll huff, and I'll puff, and I'll blow your house down," said the big bad wolf.

And sure enough, he gave a little huff, and he gave a little puff, and with very little effort he blew the house down. Before the straw had settled to the ground, the little pig ran away as fast as his little legs would carry him to the home of his nearest brother.

The next evening, just as the two brothers were sitting down at their wooden table to eat their dinner, they heard scratching and sniffing outside the house. They peeked through the wooden window and gasped in alarm when they saw the big bad wolf staring at them hungrily. His stomach rumbled loudly.

"Little piggies, little piggies, will you let me in?"

"Not on the hairs of our chinny chin chins, we will not let you in," trembled the little pigs.

"Then I'll huff, and I'll puff, and I'll blow your house down," said the big bad wolf.

And sure enough, he huffed a bit, and he puffed a bit, and with a bit of effort he blew the house down. Before the planks of wood had crashed to the ground, the two pigs ran away as fast as their little legs would carry them to the home of their brother.

The next evening, just as the three brothers were making the fire to warm their toes, they heard crunching and crashing outside the house. The third little pig pulled a tiny stone out of the wall to make a peephole, and they all shrieked in terror when they saw the big bad wolf staring at them ravenously. His stomach grumbled even louder, and he was smacking his lips with glee at the feast waiting just a short breath away!

"Little piggies, little piggies, will you let me in?"

"Not on the hairs of our chinny chin chins, we will not let you in," quaked the three little pigs.

"Then I'll huff, and I'll puff, and I'll blow your house down," said the big bad wolf.

And sure enough, he took a big huff, and he took a big puff, and with a big effort he blew. But the house didn't blow down. So he took a bigger huff, and he took a bigger puff, and with the biggest of efforts he blew. But the house still didn't blow down. So he filled his lungs as full as he could and with a mighty effort he blew and blew and blew! And the house stayed up!

With that the big bad wolf started to climb up the stone wall to the chimney on the roof. The three little pigs looked around the stark stone room and then at each other in dismay – there was nowhere in here to hide, and nowhere left to run. They would have to stand and fight the big bad wolf!

Suddenly one of the little pigs had an idea, and whispered it into the ears of his brothers. They all ran over to the fireplace and hooked a huge pot of water over the roaring fire. They heard the wolf climb into the chimney. The water in the pot started to steam. They heard the wolf climbing down the chimney. The water started to bubble. They heard the wolf slide the rest of the way down the chimney and he landed splash in the middle of the pot of now boiling water. PLOP!

"AAARRRRHHHHH!" screamed the big bad wolf, leaping immediately out of the boiling pot. The three little pigs ran around the room trying to get away from the wolf, as the big bad wolf ran around the room trying to cool down, until eventually he ran straight through the stone wall, leaving a huge big bad wolf shaped hole, and carried on running and screaming and shouting all the way through the woods. That was the last they ever saw of the big bad wolf.

The three little pigs knew they had beaten the wolf, and he would never trouble them again, so they decided to build a brand new, comfortable house to live in. They built the walls of tough, strong stone. They made tables of smooth, warm wood, and they gathered lots of sweet-smelling, soft fresh hay to make comfortable beds. It was the best house in the world, and they all lived in it happily ever after.

# *The Very Big Parcel*

Once upon a time there lived an old man and his wife. They dwelled in a small house with a small, neat garden and they were very contented. What's more, they had very good friends and neighbours, with whom they shared everything. One day, there was a knock at the door and there stood the postman with a huge parcel in his arms.

"My, oh my!" exclaimed the old man to his wife as he staggered into the kitchen with the enormous load.

"Whatever can it be?" wondered the old woman as the two of them stared at the parcel. "Perhaps it's a new set of china," said she.

"Or a new wheelbarrow," said he. And they began to think about all the fancy things there might be inside the parcel.

"Well, why don't we open it and see?" said the old lady at last. And so they did. They looked into the box and at first it seemed to be totally empty.

"Well, I never did!" cried the old man. And then he spotted something right in the corner of the box. He lifted it out into the light to examine it more carefully and discovered it was a single seed.

Well, the old man and his wife were most upset. Whereas before they were quite content, now that they had thought about all the things that might have been in the box they were bitterly disappointed by the seed. "Still," said the old man at last, "we'd better plant it anyway. Who knows, maybe we'll get a nice fresh lettuce from it."

So he planted the seed in the garden. Every day he watered the ground and soon a shoot appeared. The shoot grew into a strong young plant and then it grew taller and taller. Higher and higher it grew until it was a handsome tree. The man and his wife were excited to see fruits growing on the tree. "I wonder if they're apples," the old man said. Each day he watered the tree and examined the fruits. One day he said to his wife, "The first fruit is ready to pick." He carefully reached up into the tree and picked the large red fruit.

He and his wife frantically picked the fruits left on the tree, but when they took them indoors they found to their dismay that they were cracked and gnarled. When they broke open the fruits they were full of dust. "If only I had not been so thoughtless and remembered to water the tree!" cried the old man in anguish.

The next day the old couple looked out of the window to find that the tree had vanished. Now what were they to do? They had completely neglected to take care of their garden and now they had nothing to eat. They realised that they would have to sell their riches to buy food. Then they also needed new gardening tools, for theirs had grown rusty with neglect.

As the weeks passed, the old man and his wife gradually sold all the fine things they had bought, just to keep body and soul together. They felt truly miserable and sorry for the way they had treated their neighbours. For now they realised just how lonely they were without their friends. "We have no money now," said the wife one day, "but let's have a party anyway. For friendship is more valuable than any amount of gold coins."

So the old couple invited all their friends and neighbours round and they had a grand party. The friends wondered what had happened to all the old couple's riches and what had happened to make the old couple so friendly once more, but I don't think they ever found out, do you?

# The Lost Lion

Once there was a lion cub called Lenny. He was a very tiny lion cub, but he was sure that he was the bravest lion in all of Africa. When his mother taught her cubs how to stalk prey, Lenny would stalk his own mother and pounce on her. When she showed them how to wash themselves, Lenny licked his sister's face instead so that she growled at him. When the mother lioness led her cubs down to the watering hole to drink, he jumped into the water and created a huge splash that soaked everyone.

The other lionesses were not amused. "You'd better watch that son of yours," they said to Lenny's mother, "or he'll get into really big trouble."

One day the mother lioness led her
cubs on their first big hunt. "Stay close to me,"
she said, "or you could get hurt."
She crawled off through the undergrowth with
her cubs following on behind, one after the other. Lenny was at
the back. The grass tickled his tummy and he wanted to laugh,
but he was trying hard to be obedient. So he crawled along,
making sure he kept the bobbing tail of the cub in front in sight.
On and on they crawled until Lenny was beginning to feel quite
weary.

   "But a brave lion cub doesn't give up," he thought to himself.
And on he plodded.

   At last the grass gave way to a clearing. Lenny looked up, and to
his dismay he saw that the tail he had been following was attached,
not to one of his brothers or sisters, but to a baby elephant!

123

But the spotted shape was a cheetah! Quick as a flash, the cheetah sprang away and as he did so, his tail caught Lenny a blow that sent him spinning round and round in circles.

When Lenny stopped spinning, he got up and found that his whole body was shaking. "Oh my," he thought, "that cheetah is a fast runner." Then he added in rather a small voice, "But I'm still the bravest lion in Africa." He set off again across the plain. By now it was getting dark and Lenny was wishing he was at home with his mother and brothers and sisters. "I wonder if they've noticed I've gone," he thought sadly as a tear rolled down his furry cheek. He felt cold and tired and hungry as he crawled into the undergrowth to sleep.

Some time later Lenny was woken by a noise that was louder than anything he'd ever heard before – louder even than the elephant's trumpeting. It filled the night air and made the leaves on the trees shake. The noise was getting louder and louder and the animal that was making it was getting nearer and nearer. Lenny peeped out from his hiding place and saw a huge golden creature with big yellow eyes that shone in the dark like lamps. It had a great crown of shaggy golden fur all around its head and its red jaws were open wide revealing a set of very large white fangs. How it roared! Lenny was terrified and about to turn tail and run, when the animal stopped roaring and spoke to him. "Come here, Lenny," said the animal gently. "It's me, your father, and I'm going to take you home. Climb up on my back, little one."

So Lenny climbed up on his father's back and was carried all the way home. And when they got there his father told his mother and his brothers and sisters that Lenny had been a very brave lion after all.

# The King Who Ate Too Much

Long ago, in a kingdom far, far away, there lived a greedy king. Now the thing that this king loved, more than anything else in the whole world, was food. He simply couldn't get enough of it. Ever since he was a little prince, he had been allowed to eat whatever he wanted, whenever he wanted it. And because he was always eating, he just got fatter and fatter and fatter with every day that passed.

When he became king, his appetite seemed to get even bigger! As soon as he woke in the morning, he would have his servants bring him an enormous breakfast. After eating several huge, steaming bowls of porridge, he would eat slice after slice of hot, buttered toast and jam, followed by all the boiled eggs that the royal chickens could lay.

In case he got a little hungry mid-morning, he would have a snack – usually ten or more chocolate cakes, washed down with as many cups of tea!

At lunchtime, the table would groan with the weight of all the pies, sandwiches, fruit and biscuits that the greedy king was about to gobble down.

For afternoon tea, it would be cakes, cakes and more cakes.

But the king's biggest meal was supper! The royal cooks toiled for most of the day to prepare this feast. When it was time for the king to eat, one servant after another would carry in great bowls of steaming soup, plates of fish of every kind, followed by huge roasts and dishes of vegetables. Down it all went, followed by fruit and jelly. At last, the king would be full and he would retire to his bed for the night.

But the king's greedy eating habits also made him a very thoughtless king. No-one dared tell him that much of the wealth of the kingdom had to be spent on his huge meals. In the meantime, his loyal subjects were going hungry and becoming poor and needy.

One day, just after the king had eaten his usual big lunch, he began to feel very strange. Not only did he feel even bigger than usual, he also began to feel very light. Suddenly, without any warning, he started floating up from the table and into the air like a big balloon.

"Help! Get me down!" he cried.

130

The royal courtiers and servants jumped up and down and tried in vain to grab the king as he floated upwards, but in no time at all he had floated out of reach. Before anyone knew it, he had floated out of the castle window. Out across the royal grounds he went, over the river and towards the woods and mountains of his kingdom.

"Wooaa-aaah!" cried the king, as he disappeared from view.

Soon, the king began to float over a small farm. He looked down and saw the farmer's children, dressed only in rags, searching for firewood. Some thin, hungry cows stood nearby chewing on a few meagre pieces of hay.

Over the next farm he floated, and a similar sad scene met his gaze. Dressed in rags, a poor farmer and his family toiled their soil hoping to grow enough to eat.

Next he floated over a small village. Everywhere he looked he saw shabby, run-down houses in need of repair and people in the streets begging for money.

Every farm and every village the king floated over told the same story of hunger and misery. The king suddenly felt very sad and very ashamed. He had been so busy enjoying himself eating that he hadn't given a thought to the plight of his subjects. While he was getting fatter and fatter, they were all getting thinner and poorer.

Now, a gust of wind was blowing the king back towards his castle. As he was passing over the castle, he suddenly felt himself falling. Down, down, he went until he landed back into the castle grounds with a great thud and a bounce.

That very day, the king sent out a royal proclamation. All his loyal subjects were to come to the castle for a huge feast, after which they would all be given a purse full of gold.

As for the king, he was never greedy again. Instead of spending all his money on food for himself, he gave enough to all the people in the land so that they would never be hungry or poor again.

# The Frog Prince

There was once a king who had but one daughter. Being his only child, she wanted for nothing. She had a nursery full of toys, a pony to ride and a wardrobe bursting with pretty dresses. But, for all this, the princess was lonely. "How I wish I had someone to play with," she sighed.

The princess's favourite toy was a beautiful golden ball. Every day she would play with her ball in the palace garden. When she threw the ball up in the air, it seemed to take off of its own accord and touch the clouds before landing in the princess's hands again.

One windy day the princess was playing in the garden as usual. She threw her golden ball high into the air, but instead of returning to her hands, the wind blew the ball into the fishpond. The princess ran to the pond, but to her dismay the ball had sunk right to the bottom. "Whatever shall I do?" wailed the girl. "Now I have lost my favourite toy." And she sat down beside the pond and cried.

All at once she heard a loud PLOP! and a large green frog landed on the grass beside her. "Eeeuugh! Go away you nasty thing!" screamed the princess.

To her astonishment, the frog spoke to her. "I heard you crying," he said in a gentle voice, "and I wondered what the matter was. Can I help you in any way?"

"Yes, it is," said the princess in a small voice. And she told her father the whole story.

"When a promise is made it must be kept, my girl," said the king. "You must ask the frog to dine with you."

Presently, the frog hopped into the great hall and round to where the princess was sitting. With a great leap he was up on the table beside her. She stifled a scream.

"You promised to let me eat from your golden plate," said the frog, tucking into the princess's food. The princess felt quite sick and pushed the plate away from her. Then to her horror the frog dipped his long tongue into her golden cup and drank every drop. "It's what you promised," he reminded her.

When he had finished, the frog stretched his long, green limbs, yawned and said, "Now I feel quite sleepy. Please take me to your room."

"Do I have to?" the princess pleaded with her father.

"Yes, you do," said the king sternly. "The frog helped you when you were in need and you made him a promise."

So the princess carried the frog to her bedroom but as they reached the door she said, "My bedroom's very warm. I'm sure you'd be more comfortable out here where it's cool."

But as she opened the bedroom door, the frog leaped from her hand and landed on her bed.

"You promised that I could sleep on a silk cushion next to your bed," said the frog.

"Yes, yes, of course," said the princess looking with horror at the froggy footprints on her clean, white sheets. She called to her maid to bring a cushion.

The frog jumped on to the cushion and looked as though he was going to sleep.

"Good," thought the princess, "he's forgotten about my final promise."

But just as she was about to get into bed, he opened his eyes and said, "What about my goodnight kiss?"

"Oh, woe is me," thought the princess as she closed her eyes and pursed her lips towards the frog's cold and clammy face and kissed him.

"Open your eyes," said a voice that didn't sound a bit like the frog's. She opened her eyes and there, standing before her, was a prince. The princess stood there in dumbstruck amazement.

"Thank you," said the prince. "You have broken a spell cast upon me by a wicked witch. She turned me into a frog and said the spell would only be broken if a princess would eat with me, sleep beside me and kiss me."

They ran to tell the king what had happened. He was delighted and said, "You may live in the palace from now on, for my daughter needs a friend." And indeed, the prince and princess became the best of friends and she was never lonely again. He taught her to play football with the golden ball and she taught him to ride her pony. One day, many years later, they were married and had lots of children. And, do you know, their children were particularly good at leapfrog.

# Little Tim and His Brother Sam

Little Tim was a very lucky boy. He had a lovely home, with the nicest parents you could hope for. He had a big garden, with a swing and a football net in it. And growing in the garden were lots of trees that you could climb and have adventures in. Little Tim even had a nice school, which he enjoyed going to every day and where he had lots of friends. In fact, almost everything in Tim's life was nice. Everything that is apart from one thing – Tim's brother Sam.

Sam was a very naughty boy. Worse still, whenever he got into mischief – which he did almost all of the time – he managed to make it look as though someone else was to blame. And that someone was usually poor Tim!

Once Sam thought that he would put salt in the sugar bowl instead of sugar. That afternoon, Sam and Tim's parents had some friends round for tea. All the guests put salt in their cups of tea, of course, thinking it was sugar. Well, being very polite they didn't like to say anything, even though their cups of tea tasted very strange indeed! When Sam and Tim's parents tasted their tea, however, they guessed immediately that someone had been playing a trick. They had to apologise to their guests and make them all fresh cups of tea. And who got the blame? Little Tim did, because Sam had sprinkled salt on Tim's bedroom floor so that their mother would think that Tim was the culprit.

Another time, Sam and Tim were playing football in the garden when Sam accidentally kicked the ball against a window and broke it. Sam immediately ran away and hid, so that when their father came out to investigate, only Tim was to be seen. So poor little Tim got the blame again.

143

Then there was the time when Sam and Tim's Aunt Jessica came to stay. She was a very nice lady, but she hated anything creepy-crawly, and as far as she was concerned that included frogs. So what did Sam do? Why, he went down to the garden pond and got a big, green frog to put in Aunt Jessica's handbag. When Aunt Jessica opened her handbag to get her glasses out, there staring out of the bag at her were two froggy eyes.

"Croak!" said the frog.

"Eeek!" yelled Aunt Jessica and almost jumped out of her skin.

"I told Tim not to do it," said Sam.

Tim opened his mouth and was just about to protest his innocence when his mother said, "Tim, go to your room immediately and don't come out until you are told."

Poor Tim went to his room and had to stay there until after supper. Sam thought it was very funny.

The next day, Sam decided that he would play another prank and blame it on Tim. He went to the garden shed and, one by one, took out all the garden tools. When he thought no-one was watching, he hid them all in Tim's bedroom cupboard. In went the spade, the fork, the watering can, the trowel – in fact, everything except the lawnmower. And the only reason that the lawnmower didn't go in was because it was too heavy to carry!

But this time, Sam's little prank was about to come unstuck, for Aunt Jessica had seen him creeping up the stairs to Tim's bedroom with the garden tools. She guessed immediately what Sam was up to, and who was likely to get the blame. When Sam wasn't about, she spoke to Tim. The two of them whispered to each other for a few seconds and then smiled triumphantly.

Later that day, Sam and Tim's father went to the garden shed to do some gardening. Imagine his surprise when all he saw were some old flower pots and the lawnmower. He searched high and low for the garden tools. He looked behind the compost heap, under the garden steps, behind the sand pit and in the garage. But they weren't anywhere to be seen.

Then he started searching in the house. He looked in the kitchen cupboard, and was just looking under the stairs when something at the top of the stairs caught his eye. The handle from the garden spade was sticking out of the door to Sam's bedroom. Looking rather puzzled, he went upstairs and walked into Sam's bedroom. There, nestling neatly in the cupboard, were the rest of the tools.

"Sam, come up here immediately," called his father.

Sam, not realising anything was amiss, came sauntering upstairs. Suddenly he saw all the garden tools that he had so carefully hidden in Tim's cupboard now sitting in *his* cupboard. He was speechless.

"Right," said his father, "before you go out to play, you can take all the tools back down to the garden shed. Then you can cut the grass. Then you can dig over the flower beds, and then you can do the weeding."

Well, it took Sam hours to do all the gardening. Tim and Aunt Jessica watched from the window and clutched their sides with laughter. Sam never did find out how all the garden tools found their way into his bedroom, but I think you've guessed, haven't you?

# The Missing Scarf

Kanga was very proud of her stripy knitted scarf. She had made it herself and she had also made a smaller matching one for her son, Joey. Kanga used to hop through the bush with her scarf streaming out behind her, while Joey's could just be seen poking out of the top of her pouch. Now Joey was older, he was too big for Kanga's pouch, but he still wore his scarf as he hopped along beside his mother.

Then one day Kanga woke up to find that her beautiful scarf was missing. She searched high and low but it was nowhere to be found. Eventually she decided that she would have to go out into the bush to look for it.

"Stay here," she said to Joey. "I'll try not to be long. I'm sure to find my scarf soon." Kanga hopped off into the bush and started to search among the roots of trees and under stones.

She had gone quite a long way when, looking up into the branches of a eucalyptus tree, she spotted Koala. Now Koala was usually to be found asleep, but this time she was busy preparing a meal of eucalyptus leaves for her children. Kanga looked up at Koala and then her jaw dropped. For Koala was quite clearly wearing Kanga's scarf around her tummy. Then, to Kanga's horror, she saw Koala use the end of the scarf to wipe the teacups! "Koala," Kanga called. "Whatever do you think you're doing?"

Koala stopped cleaning the teacups and looked down through the branches of the eucalyptus tree at Kanga. "I'm wiping my teacups with my apron," she replied sleepily, "and I'll thank you not to interfere!" And with that, she yawned and moved several branches further up the tree.

149

Poor Kanga felt very embarrassed. How could she have mistaken Koala's striped apron for her own scarf? She hopped away and carried on further into the bush. After a while she could hear Kookaburra's familiar laughing call nearby. "I know," thought Kanga, "I'll ask her if she's seen my scarf. She'd be able to spot it easily from up in the sky." She followed the sound of Kookaburra's call until she came to the tree where she lived. She looked up and, sure enough, there was Kookaburra flying towards the tree. Kanga was about to call up when her jaw dropped again. For Kookaburra was quite clearly carrying Kanga's scarf in her beak. "Kookaburra," Kanga called. "Whatever do you think you're doing?"

"I'm lining my nest," mumbled Kookaburra through a beakful of stripy feathers. "And I'll thank you not to interfere," she added more distinctly, for she had now reached the nest and was arranging the feathers carefully in place.

150

Poor Kanga felt even more embarrassed. How could she have mistaken the feathers for her own scarf? She hopped away and carried on further into the bush. After a while she reached a wide open plain and there she saw Emu running past with his baby chicks on his back. As he rushed past, Kanga's jaw dropped yet again. For Emu quite clearly had Kanga's scarf tucked in among his chicks. "Emu," called Kanga. "Whatever do you think you're doing?"

"I'm taking my chicks to safety," said Emu, glancing up at the sky as he sped away. "And you'd be wise to do the same," he added. Then Kanga realised that what she had thought was her rolled-up scarf were just the striped chicks on Emu's back.

Poor Kanga felt even more embarrassed. How could she have made such a mistake? Then she felt a few spots of rain on her nose and, looking up, saw a huge black cloud overhead. There was no time to lose – she must find shelter.

She made a dash for some trees at the edge of the plain and soon found herself by a stream. She wandered along beside the stream feeling cold, wet, tired and miserable. Finally, she lay down in the wet grass beside the stream and tried to get to sleep. She shivered with cold and wondered how Joey was and whether he was behaving himself. She so hoped he hadn't got into mischief.

Just then there was a tap on her shoulder and there stood Platypus. "I could hear you in my burrow over there," she said pointing towards a hole beside the stream just above the water. "I thought you might like this to keep you warm," she added.

"My scarf!" exclaimed Kanga.

"Oh, is that what it is? I'm ever so sorry," said Platypus. "I've been using it as a blanket for my babies. It's rather cold and damp in my burrow, you know," she added, rather forlornly.

"Where did you find it?" asked Kanga.

"It was stuck on some thorns and I know I shouldn't have taken it, but I just thought it would be so nice for keeping my

152

young ones warm," blurted Platypus, and she started to sob.

"There now," said Kanga, "don't cry. You can keep the scarf. You need it more than me."

Platypus stopped crying and looked overjoyed. "Thank you," she said.

"No, thank you," said Kanga. "I've learned a lesson, which is not to get upset over a scarf, for I've ended up falling out with my friends."

Kanga made her way back home, but it took a long time because she apologised to all her friends on the way. When she explained what had happened Emu, Kookaburra and Koala all forgave her, and by the time she reached home she was feeling much better. Joey was there to greet her. "What have you been up to while I was away?" she asked.

"I made you this," he said. He handed her a scarf. It was a very funny-looking scarf, made out of twigs, grass and feathers, but Kanga loved it very much.

"This is much more special than my old scarf," she said. And she gave Joey an extra big hug.

153

# Lucy and the Green Door

Lucy Jenkins lived in an ordinary house, in an ordinary street, in an ordinary town. At the back of Lucy's house was an ordinary garden with ordinary flowers and an ordinary path. But down the path at the bottom of the garden was a tree that was not ordinary at all! It was a huge old oak tree, and at the bottom of the tree was a very small green door, only just big enough for Lucy to squeeze through. This was Lucy's secret, because only she knew about the door. But what lay behind the door was Lucy's best secret of all!

Each afternoon Lucy would go down the garden path and knock lightly on the door. On the third knock the door would swing open wide, and the chief elf would be there to welcome her inside.

"Come inside, little Lucy," the elf would always say, "and have some tea."

Inside, Lucy would meet some very special friends indeed! First there were Penelope and Geraldine, two of the gentlest and sweetest fairies it was possible to imagine. Then there were Basil and Granville, who were rather mischievous imps (but who made Lucy laugh with their tricks and jokes), and there were the storytellers, who would sit for hours with Lucy and tell her the greatest tales from all the corners of the world. And of course there was the chief elf, who would make the most delicious milkshakes and scones with heaps of cream for Lucy to eat.

The world behind the green door was a wonderful place, and Lucy would always go home afterwards feeling very cheerful and jolly. On one particular visit to the world behind the green door Lucy had just finished a scrumptious tea of cocoa and toasted marshmallows with the chief elf, when she went off to play games with Basil and Granville. They were playing blind man's buff, and Lucy roared with laughter as Basil sneaked up on the blindfolded Granville and tickled him in the ribs, making him squeal and beg for the teasing to stop.

155

Now just recently, Lucy had been feeling down in the dumps because very soon she would be going to school and would only be able to visit her friends at weekends. But they assured her that they would never forget her, and that as long as she was always a true friend to them she could visit as often or as little as she liked. This cheered Lucy up considerably, and then they took her to visit the storytellers so that her happiness was complete. Of all the delights behind the green door, the storytellers were Lucy's favourite. They told her stories of how the whales had learned to sing, and of where the stars went when the sun had risen in the sky and they had slipped from view.

Because of the assurances of the fairies, Lucy was not too worried when the day finally came for her to join all the other boys and girls of her age at school. Every day, Lucy would go to school and then afterwards would visit her friends behind the green door. As winter came round and the days grew dark she only visited at weekends, and looked forward to the holidays when she could visit them every day once more.

Meanwhile, at school, Lucy had made friends with a girl called Jessica, and although she told Jessica all about her family and her home, she didn't at first tell her about her extraordinary tree with the little green door and the magic world that lay beyond. Lucy did tell Jessica all the stories that she was told by the storytellers, however, and Jessica grew more and more curious about where she had heard all the wonderful tales. Every day, Jessica would ask more and more questions, and Lucy found it more and more difficult to avoid telling her about her secret. Eventually, Lucy gave in and told Jessica all about her adventures behind the green door.

Jessica scoffed and laughed when Lucy told her about the chief elf, and Basil, Granville, Penelope and Geraldine. She howled with laughter at the thought of the wonderful teas and the stories that followed. Jessica thought that Lucy was making the whole thing up! When Lucy protested, and said it was true, Jessica told her that it simply wasn't possible – that there were no such things as elves and fairies and imps and strange and wonderful worlds behind doors in trees. Lucy was distraught, and decided to take Jessica to the green door.

On the way home Lucy started to worry. What if she really had imagined it all? But if her wonderful friends didn't exist, how could she possibly know them? Jessica walked beside Lucy, still teasing her and laughing about Lucy's 'invisible' friends!

When Lucy and Jessica reached the bottom of the garden, Lucy was about to tap lightly on the green door at the bottom of the oak tree when she suddenly noticed the door had disappeared. She rubbed her eyes and looked again, but it simply wasn't there!

Jessica smirked and laughed at Lucy, calling her silly and babyish to believe in magic and fairy tales, and then ran off back down the road to school. Lucy could not face going back to school that afternoon, and when her mother saw her enter the house she thought she must be ill – she looked so upset! Lucy went to bed early and cried herself to sleep.

And when Lucy slept she started to dream. The chief elf, Basil and Granville, Penelope and Geraldine and the storytellers were all there in the dream. Then Penelope and Geraldine stepped forward and hugged Lucy, and the hug was so real that

Lucy began to hope it wasn't a dream! Then they all hugged her and asked why she hadn't been to see them for so long, and why they had not been able to reach out to her except now in the deepest of sleeps. Lucy explained what had happened on her last visit, and told them all about Jessica, and then Geraldine spoke. "Little Lucy," she said, "you are special. You believe in magic and you believe in the little people. And because you believe, you are able to see us and live among us. But those who don't believe will always be shut out from our world. You must keep your belief, little Lucy."

With a huge surge of happiness Lucy woke up, dressed quickly and ran out of her ordinary house, down the ordinary path in the ordinary garden up to the extraordinary tree, and was delighted to see the green door once more! She knocked very lightly and, after the third tap, the door swung open to reveal the chief elf. "Come inside, little Lucy," the elf said happily, "and have some tea."

# The Sleeping Beauty

A long time ago, in a land far away, there ruled the happiest king and queen who had ever lived. They were especially happy because after years of hoping in vain, they had finally been blessed by the birth of a beautiful baby daughter.

The king and queen were so happy that they decided to celebrate by throwing a huge banquet for their family and friends, and all the most important people in the kingdom. As they sat down to write the invitations, a worried look crossed the queen's face. "The Countess Griselda will be very angry if she doesn't get an invitation," she said to her husband.

The king's face went very pale for a moment. Then he shook his head and said, "No, she must not be invited. Griselda is wicked and mean. I do not wish her to cast her eyes on our beautiful daughter." With that they continued writing the invitations.

The day of the banquet arrived, and all the most important people took their places in the Great Hall. Before the celebrations began, a line formed to pay homage to the little Princess Angelina, who lay sleeping in her cradle next to the king and queen's thrones. Twelve people stood in line, and one by one they stepped forward to give their gift to the sleeping princess.

First up stepped the good Lady Soprano, who touched the baby's throat with her forefinger and declared that the princess would have a voice like an angel. Next came the Archduke Ernest, and with a light touch on her forehead he vowed she would grow to be very wise. Next came the Duchess Rose, who stroked the baby's face and declared she would blossom into the most beautiful flower in the kingdom.

161

One by one the guests came forward and bestowed the gifts of patience, kindness, faith, grace, fortune, virtue, happiness and sweetness. With just one guest left to give her gift, there was a terrible noise outside the Great Hall and the huge doors were thrown open in a rage. In stormed the Countess Griselda. The Great Hall fell silent as she slowly approached the sleeping baby. The king and queen jumped to their feet to protect their little one, but Griselda swept them both aside.

As they looked up in fear at Griselda, she turned to them and whispered in a hard, cruel voice, "I think you mislaid my invitation, but I have come to give my gift to the precious child anyway." As she bent over the child she cackled, "To this child I bestow the gift of absolute health until the day she dies." As relief showed itself on the faces of the crowd, she roared with laughter and bellowed, "Which is why it is such a pity she will not live beyond her sixteenth birthday!" The crowd was stunned as she continued, "A spindle shall be her end. A common peasant's spindle." And she touched the tip of the middle finger on the baby's right hand. She then clapped her hands together and a great roll of thunder was heard, before a terrible wind swept through the open doors blowing out all the candles. When the doors were shut and the candles re-lit, Griselda had disappeared, leaving only her terrible spell behind her.

As the king and queen wept, they did not see the final guest who had yet to bestow her gift. The Marquess Maria bent over Angelina and whispered, "I cannot take away the evil of Griselda, but I can give you the greatest gift of all. I give you the gift of love. On that terrible day to come you shall not die a death, but sleep, little one, sleep deep and peacefully as you sleep now, until love comes to rescue you." She placed her forefinger on the baby's heart and then was gone.

The king and queen were in despair, and they demanded that every spindle in the kingdom be destroyed. But they couldn't sleep a single night without worrying, and a day didn't pass that they let the little princess out of their sight for a moment.

Angelina grew, and with every passing year she became sweeter, and with every passing day she became more beautiful.

163

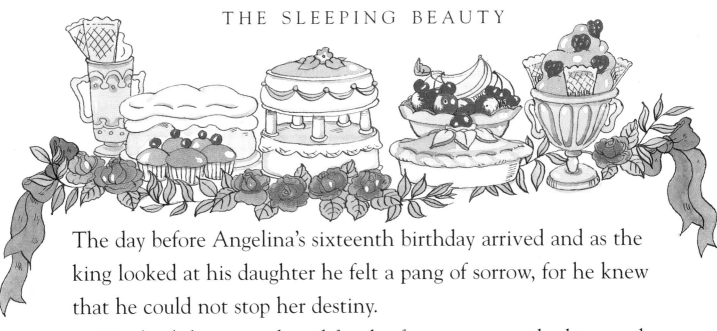

The day before Angelina's sixteenth birthday arrived and as the king looked at his daughter he felt a pang of sorrow, for he knew that he could not stop her destiny.

Her birthday arrived, and for the first time ever the king and queen allowed her to roam freely around the castle. The king had ordered a huge celebration to be prepared in the Great Hall for later in the day, and Angelina had tremendous fun watching the cooks prepare delicious pies, pastries and cakes in the kitchens. She watched the servants making garlands of flowers and roamed through all the corridors to watch the preparations.

In a corridor off the Great Hall, she followed a trail of petals, winding first one way and then another, up and up into a turret in the castle that she had never visited before. When she reached the top, a door swung open and in the corner of the darkened room a little old lady sat spinning some yarn.

"Come closer, my child," she beckoned.

Angelina moved closer.

"Closer still," she urged.

When Angelina was close enough the old woman

164

reached out to Angelina's right hand and pulled it to the spindle needle. The princess gave a gasp of pain as it pricked her middle finger, and then she fell into the deepest, most peaceful of sleeps. And as she fell asleep, the whole castle fell asleep, too. The cooks fell asleep at the roasting spit. The horses fell asleep in the stable. The king fell asleep on his throne. Everything in the castle came to a complete and utter standstill.

The years passed by, and with every passing year the thorns that grew around the castle became thicker and higher, and the legend of the sleeping beauty spread to distant lands. As time went on, many brave princes tried to cut down the thorns, but not one succeeded and countless young men were lost forever in the forest of thorns.

Many years had passed before one brave prince awoke from a dream in which the angelic voice of a strange girl had called to him from a thorn bush. He asked his father the meaning of the dream, but the king shook his head and said it was best he didn't know.

But the following night, the young prince once again dreamed of the strange girl, and this time he saw the princess deep in sleep but calling to be freed. The prince was enchanted. She was the most beautiful girl he had ever seen, and again he asked his father who she was. Again the king refused to say anything, but when the prince's dreams continued and the prince felt he would rather die than live without the princess, the king relented, and told his son of the sleeping princess far, far away.

The prince lost no time, and set off on a voyage that lasted a year and a day. Along the way he heard tales of the princes who had tried before him and the fate they had met; some had been turned to stone, some had turned to water, and others had simply vanished without trace, but none had succeeded.

The prince finally reached his destination and stood outside the walls of the thorn forest. He knelt and said a prayer for all the lost souls who had tried before him, and then he raised his sword to strike the thorns. In that instant, a vision of the princess rose up to him, and he was so overcome with love that he dropped his sword and tried to touch the vision. As he reached out he touched the thorns, and as he touched the thorns, they turned into flowers in his hands. The further into the forest he went, the more the forest bowed down before him, until all that separated him from the princess was a carpet of roses. The prince raced past the sleeping horses, cooks and the king and ran up the stairs to where the princess lay. He bent over her sleeping form and placed a single kiss upon her rosy lips. In that instant, she opened her eyes – love had set her free.

The cooks yawned at their spit and woke up. The horses neighed their yawns and woke up. The king yawned on his throne and woke up. Everyone in the castle woke up. When the prince led the princess to her father he cried with joy, and granted him any wish that he could choose. The prince asked for the princess's hand in marriage, and they both lived happily ever after.

# The Singing Bear

Long ago, there lived a young boy named Peter. He was a gentle lad who loved all creatures, but most of all he loved the animals and birds of the forest. Many a time he had mended a jay's broken wing, or set a badger free from a cruel trap.

One day, the fair came to town and Peter was very excited. He could see brightly coloured tents being put up in the field and carts arriving with mysterious looking loads. As soon as the fair was open Peter was off with his penny in his pocket to try his luck. First of all he had a go at the coconut shy. Then he tried to climb the greasy pole. Finally, he used his last farthing on the tombola stall. He was about to head for home when out of the corner of his eye he caught a glimpse of a dreadful sight. Lying in a cage, looking sad and forlorn, was a large brown bear. On a small plate at the front of the cage was the bear's name: Lombard. He looked so dejected that Peter immediately vowed to set him free. The cage was strongly padlocked and Peter knew not how he could break the lock. He turned to make his way home, with the bear gazing pitifully after him.

That night, Peter tossed and turned in his bed. What was he to do? He wasn't strong enough to break into the bear's cage and his keeper would surely not agree to set him free. In the middle of the night, he resolved to return to the fairground to comfort the bear.

He slipped out of bed and made his way by the light of the moon back to the fairground. To his astonishment he found the bear singing a song to himself in a beautiful voice. For a while Peter listened to the lovely sound of the bear's singing. Then he had an idea. He remembered a piece of paper he had seen pinned to the palace gate.

"Don't cry, Lombard," he said. "I think I know a way to get you out of here. But first you must teach me your song." The bear was happy to oblige and soon the two of them were singing the song together. Then Peter said, "I must go, but I'll be back tomorrow. And remember, when you see me, be ready to sing your song."

The next day, Peter put on his very best clothes and set off for the palace. Pinned to the gate was the piece of paper, just as Peter had remembered. On the paper was written in a handsome script: *The King Requires a Minstrel with a Fine Voice. Apply Within.*

Peter knocked at the gate. He was shown into a beautiful golden gallery where a row of minstrels were waiting to be auditioned. A courtier rang a little bell for silence, and in came the king. He sat down at his great gold throne.

"Let the audition begin," cried the king. The first minstrel stepped forward. He sang a song in a sweet, high voice that tugged at the heart and reduced the court to tears. The next minstrel sang in a deep, rich voice that sent shivers down the spine, so that the birds in the trees stopped singing to listen. The next minstrel sang a song that was so witty and amusing that the entire court wept with laughter.

At last it was Peter's turn. He stepped forward, gave a deep bow and said, "I beg your majesty's permission to perform my song out of doors, so that all the wild creatures of the forest might hear it, too."

"What a strange request!" said the king. However, if the truth be told, he had grown quite sleepy listening to so many beautiful songs and thought the fresh air might liven him up. "Very well, but it had better be worth it!" he said, giving Peter a fierce look.

"Follow me!" called Peter. He led the king, the court and all the minstrels out of the palace gates and down the road.

"Where are we going?" and "This is very untoward," they muttered. At last they reached the fairground, but Peter didn't stop until he was in view of Lombard's cage. Lombard saw him and Peter winked at the bear.

"This is where I'd like to sing for you," said Peter to the king.

The king's royal eyebrows rose higher and higher as he looked around him. "Well, I must say this is very odd indeed! However, as we've come this far, we may as well hear your song. Proceed!" said the king.

Peter opened his mouth and mimed the words while Lombard sang. It was the most beautiful song that anyone had ever heard. By the end of the song, the king was sobbing tears of joy, mirth and sorrow all together.

"That was the finest song I ever heard," he said. "You have won the audition and I would like you to be my minstrel."

Peter took another low bow. "Sire," he said. "Would that I could accept, but in all honesty it was not I who sang but my friend, Lombard the bear." Everyone gasped as they saw the bear in his cage.

For a moment the king looked furious. But then he began to smile and said, "I praise you for your honesty, Peter, and I would very much like to have Lombard for my minstrel. Chancellor, bring me the royal purse."

The king paid Lombard's keeper handsomely, who was then delighted to set the bear free. Lombard became the king's minstrel and was famous throughout the land, and from then on Peter went to the palace each day and sang duets with his friend, the bear. And it is said that, in the end, Peter married the king's daughter.

# The Princess and the Snowman

One morning Princess Bella looked out of her bedroom window and saw that the palace was covered in a thick layer of snow. Snow lay on the turrets and along the tops of the walls. There was snow in the well and snow on the guards' hats. The palace garden was so deep with snow it looked as though it was covered in delicious icing. The snow looked fresh, inviting and untouched – apart from a line of paw prints made by Bella's pet cat, Beau.

The princess clapped her hands with glee. "I'm going to make a snowman," she cried, and rushed off to find her warmest coat and gloves. Soon she was busy in the garden rolling a great ball of snow for the snowman's body and another one for his head.

At last the snowman was finished, and she put an old hat on his head and a scarf around his neck.

"Now," thought Princess Bella, "he needs a face." Turning to Beau she said, "Go and find the snowman a nose."

"Meiow!" said Beau and trotted off. Bella found three lumps of coal and stuck them in a row on the snowman's head to make a mouth. Then she stuck a stone on each side of his head for ears. Beau came back with a piece of carrot in her mouth.

"Well done, Beau," said Bella. "That's perfect for a nose." And she stuck the carrot in place.

At that moment there was a call from a palace window. "Bella, Bella! Come inside at once. It's time for your lessons," called the queen. Bella ran indoors and, do you know, she forgot all about giving the snowman a pair of eyes.

"I wonder when the princess will come and give me my eyes," thought the snowman wistfully. "I'd better keep my wits about me." He listened hard with his stone ears and sniffed with his carrot nose, but there was no-one there.

Night came and all the lights in the palace went out. In the middle of the night, a storm blew up. The windows of the palace rattled, the trees creaked and groaned and the wind moaned. The snowman strained his stone ears even harder and now he could hear a fearsome icy jangle and a piercing, shrieking laugh. It was the Ice Queen. As she blew past the snowman, he felt the Ice Queen's cold breath on his snowy cheek and the touch of her icicle fingers on his snowy brow. The snowman shivered with fear. Now he heard the Ice Queen's icy tap, tap, tap on the palace door and her howl as she slipped through the keyhole. There was silence for a while, then suddenly the snowman heard a window being flung open and the Ice Queen's cruel laugh.

"She's leaving," thought the snowman with relief.

But what was this? Now he could hear the sound of a girl sobbing and as the Ice Queen passed he heard

176

Princess Bella's voice calling, "Help me!" Then there was silence again, save for the sound of the wind in the trees.

"She's carried off the princess," thought the snowman. "There's only one thing to do!" He drew his breath and with all his might he shouted through his coal lips, "Heeelp!" He thought to himself, "No-one will hear my shouts above the noise of the wind."

But soon he felt a warm glow on his cheek. "Can I help?" said a soft, kindly voice. "I am the South Wind and I can see you're in trouble."

The snowman could hardly believe his stone ears. "Oh, yes, please help," he cried. "The Ice Queen has carried off Princess Bella and I'm afraid she may die of cold."

"I'll see what I can do," said the South Wind gently, and she started to blow a warm wind. She blew and she blew and soon the Ice Queen's icy arms began to melt. Then Bella was able to slip from her cold grasp.

"It was the snowman who saved you," whispered the South Wind in Bella's ear as she carried her back to the palace.

Bella could hear the drip, drip, sound of snow being melted by the South Wind's warm breath. As she reached the palace gate, the sun was rising and the snow in the garden was turning to slush. "I must see my snowman before he is gone," she thought.

There he was on the lawn. His hat was starting to slide off his head and his mouth was all crooked. She rushed over to him and to her astonishment he spoke.

"Please give me my eyes before I melt completely," he begged.

"Yes, of course I will," Bella replied. Quickly she fixed two pieces of coal in place on his melting face.

"You are so lovely," said the snowman, looking at her with his coal eyes. "I have one last request before I'm gone. Will you marry me?"

"Why, I will!" said Bella without thinking twice – for how could she refuse the request of the one who had saved her from the Ice Queen?

Bella could not bear to think that the snowman was melting away. She glanced down so that he would not see that she was crying.

"Bella," he said. She looked up and there standing before her was a prince. For once in her life she was speechless.

"Long ago, the Ice Queen carried me away – just like she did to you. She cast a spell on me that meant I could only return to earth as falling snow. But by agreeing to marry me you have broken the spell," said the prince.

And so Bella and the prince were married, and lived happily ever after.

# The Golden Bird

There was once a king who kept a golden bird in a gilded cage. The bird wanted for nothing. Every day the king's servant brought him food and water and groomed his fine yellow feathers. And each day the bird sang his beautiful song for the king. "How lucky I am," cried the king, "to have such a beautiful bird that sings such a fine song." However, as time passed the king began to feel sorry for the bird. "It really isn't fair," he thought, "to keep such a handsome creature in a cage. I must give the bird its freedom." He called his servant and ordered him to take the cage into the jungle and release the bird.

180

The servant obeyed, and took the cage deep into the jungle where he came to a small clearing. He set the cage down, opened the door and out hopped the golden bird. "I hope you can look after yourself," the servant said as he walked away.

The golden bird looked about him. "This is strange!" he thought to himself. "Still, I suppose someone will come along to feed me soon." He settled down and waited.

After a while he heard a crashing sound in the trees, and then he saw a monkey swinging from branch to branch on his long arms.

"Hello there!" called the monkey, hanging by his tail and casting the bird an upside down grin. "Who are you?"

"I am the golden bird," replied the golden bird haughtily.

"I can see you're new around here," said the monkey. "I'll show you the best places to feed in the tree tops."

181

"No thanks," replied the golden bird ungratefully. "What could an ape like you possibly teach me? You've got such a funny face. I expect you're envious of my beautiful beak," he added.

"Have it your own way," called the monkey as he swung off into the trees.

Some time later the golden bird heard a hissing noise in the undergrowth and a snake came slithering by. "Well, hello," hissed the snake. "Who are you?"

"I am the golden bird," replied the golden bird proudly.

"Let me show you the jungle paths," said the snake.

"No thanks," replied the bird rudely. "What could a snake possibly teach me? With your horrid hissing voice, you must be jealous of my beautiful song," he said, forgetting that he had not opened his beak to sing yet.

"Very well," hissed the snake as he slithered away into the undergrowth.

By now the golden bird was beginning to wonder when his food would arrive. He began to imagine the tasty morsel that he hoped he would soon be eating. Just then he was aware of a movement on the tree trunk behind him. Looking up he caught a glimpse of a chameleon, lying camouflaged against the trunk.

"Good day," said the chameleon. "I've been here all the time, so I know who you are. You're the golden bird. I've heard you say it twice. It's a good idea to know where to hide in case of danger. Let me show you."

"No thanks," replied the golden bird. "What could an ugly brute like you possibly teach me? You must wish you had lovely feathers like me," he said, fluffing up his beautiful, golden plumage.

"Don't say I didn't warn you," muttered the chameleon as he darted away.

183

The golden bird had just settled down again when a great grey shadow passed over the jungle. He looked up to see an eagle swooping low over the trees. The monkey swung up to hide in the densest foliage near the top of the trees. The snake slid into the deepest part of the undergrowth. The chameleon stayed quite still but his skin colour became a perfect match for the tree he was on and he became totally invisible.

"Aha!" thought the golden bird. "All I have to do is fly away and that stupid eagle will never catch up with me." He flapped his wings and flapped and flapped, but he did not know that his wings had grown weak through living a life of luxury in the palace. Now the bird regretted his golden plumage and wished that he had dull brown feathers that would not show up in the forest clearing. For his fine yellow feathers made him easy to see. He was sure the eagle would come and gobble him up. "Help!" he trilled. "Please help me someone." Now he could see the eagle swooping down towards him with eyes blazing like fire and talons drawn.

At that moment the golden bird felt something close around his legs and pull him into the undergrowth. It was the snake. Then he was lifted up into the trees by a long, hairy arm and saw he was being carried by the monkey. "Keep still," whispered the chameleon pushing him into the centre of a large yellow flower. "The eagle won't see you there." And sure enough, the golden bird found that he was precisely the colour of the flower and the eagle flew straight past him.

"However can I repay you all?" exclaimed the bird. "You saved my life!"

"You can sing for us," replied the animals. And from then on, the monkey, the snake and the chameleon looked after the golden bird, and he sang his beautiful song for them every day.

# The Magic Tree

Tommy rubbed his eyes, blinked hard, and looked out of his bedroom window again. But it was still there – an enormous oak tree that definitely hadn't been there yesterday! If it had been there, he'd have known all about it for sure. For a start he would have climbed up it, for Tommy loved nothing better than climbing trees.

No, this tree was definitely not there yesterday! Tommy sat staring at the tree in wonder and disbelief. The tree stood there, outside his bedroom window, with its huge, spreading branches almost asking to be climbed. Tommy wondered how on earth it had suddenly got there, but he decided that before he wondered about that too much, he had better go and climb it first. After all, there was always time later to wonder about things but never enough time to do things, he thought.

As soon as he was dressed, he ran outside to take a closer look at the new tree. It seemed just like any other big oak tree. It had lots of wide, inviting branches and lots of green, rounded leaves. And it had deep, furrowed bark just like any other oak tree.

Tommy couldn't resist any longer. On to the lowest branch he stepped and then up to the next. The tree seemed so easy to climb. There were branches everywhere. In no time at all, he was in a green, leafy canopy. He couldn't even see the ground any more. But something seemed not quite right. The branches beneath his feet seemed to be so big now that he could stand up on them and walk in any direction. And the branches all around him seemed just like trees themselves. In fact, he suddenly realised that he wasn't any longer climbing a tree, but standing in a whole forest full of trees.

187

Tommy didn't like this at all, and thought he had better get down. But where was down? All he could see were tall, swaying trees and here and there a twisty path leading off even deeper into the forest. Tommy didn't know how he had done it, but he had somehow got himself completely lost in a forest, and he hadn't even had breakfast yet!

Worse still, it seemed to be getting dark. "Quick, over here!" a voice suddenly called out. Tommy was very startled, but he was even more startled when he saw that the voice belonged to a squirrel.

"You can speak!" blurted out Tommy.

"Of course I can speak!" snapped the squirrel. "Now listen. You are in great danger, and there's no time to lose if we are to save you from the clutches of the evil Wizard of the Woods."

The squirrel quickly explained that, long ago, a spell had been cast on the forest and it had become enchanted. Every now and again, the Wizard of the Woods, who ruled the forest, lured an unsuspecting person into his realm by making a tree appear. Once you climbed the tree, you entered the forest. Escape was almost impossible.

"But why does the Wizard of the Woods want to lure people into the forest?" asked Tommy, rather hoping that he didn't have to hear the answer.

"To turn them into fertilizer to make the trees grow," said the squirrel.

Tommy didn't really know what fertilizer was, but it sounded rather nasty. He was pleased when the squirrel suddenly said, "There is just one way to get you out of here. But we must hurry. Soon it will be dark and the Wizard of the Woods will awake. Once he awakes, he will smell your blood and he will capture you."

With that, the squirrel jumped up the nearest tree. "Follow me," he said.

Tommy immediately climbed after the squirrel. "Where are we going?" he panted as they climbed higher and higher.

"To the top of the tallest tree in the forest," the squirrel answered as they clambered from tree to tree, climbing ever higher.

"But why?" asked Tommy.

"Because that's the only way to escape. You'll see!" said the squirrel.

Eventually they stopped climbing. They were at the top of the tallest tree in the forest. Below them and around them was nothing but more trees. Tommy looked up, and at last he could see the clear, twilight sky. He also noticed something rather strange. All the leaves at the top of the tallest tree were enormous.

"Quick, time is running out," said the squirrel. "Sit on this leaf and hold tight."

Tommy sat on one of the huge leaves. The squirrel whistled, and before Tommy could blink he had been joined by a hundred more squirrels. They each took hold of the branch to which the leaf was attached. With a great heave, they pulled and pulled until the branch was bent backwards. Suddenly they let go. With a mighty "TWANG", the branch, with Tommy and the leaf attached, sprang forward. As it did so Tommy and the leaf were launched into the air. High above the trees they soared until, ever so slowly, they began to float down to earth. Down, down, they went, until they landed with a bump.

Tommy opened his eyes to find himself on his bedroom floor. He ran over to the window and looked out. The magic tree was nowhere to be seen. It had gone as quickly as it had appeared. But perhaps it had never been there at all. Maybe it was just a dream. What do you think?